Nothing's Mat

Nothing's
Mat
a novel

ERNA
BRODBER

The University of the West Indies Press

Jamaica • Barbados • Trinidad and Tobago

The University of the West Indies Press
7A Gibraltar Hall Road, Mona
Kingston 7, Jamaica
www.uwipress.com

A catalogue record of this book is available
from the National Library of Jamaica.

ISBN: 978-976-640-494-9 (print)
978-976-640-500-7 (Kindle)
978-976-640-501-4 (ePub)

Book and cover design by Robert Harris
Set in Dante 11/14.5 x 27
Printed in the United States of America

contents

part 1.

1. making the mat

My people in the long-ago, according to my father, were very keen on manners and respect, usually from the young to the old, so a handle had to be put on the first name of the older ones. It got so ridiculous that you had people called Uncle Brother. This adult male might have been called "Brother" as a pet name by his younger sibs and gone into life as a man called Brother. The ordinary young could not call this adult male Brother. That was disrespect. You had to put a handle to his name, thus a nephew would call him "Uncle Brother" and his nephews' age-mates would call him Mr Brother or Mass Brother.

In like manner I was introduced in absentia to an old lady whom I was instructed to call "Conut". "Co" I knew to be the abbreviated form of "cousin". She was my cousin, I assumed, many stages removed. It never struck me to ask what "Nut" represented. It was in the usual eavesdropping on adults, who when they are out of the sight of children feel they can relax and call things by their real name, that I discovered that "Nut" was the shortened form of "Nothing". And the lady was really Cousin Nothing, contracted to Conut. My mother for some reason found her name and/ or her being a great thing with which to tease my father; she could crack her sides with laughter by just saying "Cousin Nothing". Conut was on his side of the family. Little bits from my grandfather and grandmother when

Conut was in one of her deathbed episodes, and I was visiting, filled out the story of Cousin Nothing's name.

Though I was wrapped in several names – all of us in my family, on both sides were – you could shake them out and find your formal name: Jean, John named after an ancestor, named because somebody liked the sound of the word; a major character in the book she was reading before your mother went into labour or your grandmother's favourite character in the Bible. Then there were additional names. These were "pet" or home names. Your formal name was private. Any and anybody ought not to be bawling it out on the street. It was for official occasions.

Pet names came from how you looked when you were born. "Tiny" was a common one and it was really amusing to see a big buxom woman like my aunt, my mother's sister, called that. This pet name often was not an English word; more likely than not, it was a set of syllables put together, like "Bludum", which came to somebody's mind when they first saw the baby, and those syllables stuck. How does someone come to be called "Nothing" and so totally that nobody can quickly find the formal name? I didn't ask anyone. I just pondered. Nine from eight, you can't. Go into the tens line and borrow one. Add that to the nine and it becomes eighteen. Nine from eighteen, you can. It leaves nine. That was arithmetic of my father's time and which he had tried to teach me. Nine from nine leaves nothing. Did Conut's name have something to do with her approach to arithmetic?

Conut and the origin of her name come back to me as at thirty, the age of the old maid, I sit on my daybed and contemplate the hills coming in through the glass windows and doors. I feel like nothing. The Conut I first met was ancient from the perspective of my seventeen-year-old sense of things, but her eyes danced and, though she was perfectly toothless, she could turn a tune, and apparently wanted to, for she did sing. There was something happening in Conut's head. Nothing is happening in mine except for a slight pain which is linked to nothing, not to an exposed nerve in a tooth, not to an overworked optical nerve, not to clogged sinuses. I know this, for I have just had what they call in the medical field an "executive profile" and been declared healthy. All I have in my head is a slight pain, there by itself, for it is linked to no other part of my system. I therefore cannot diagnose and treat: I must leave my slight pain hanging there.

My stomach rumbles and I go to the toilet expectantly: something pleasant will happen. Nothing. Not even the goat-like substance which my doctor tells me is the hallmark of constipation. My parts are not speaking to each other, but thank God this situation sparks a memory. My frontal lobe is intact, so I am still human, but I remind myself that elephants too are said to be good at remembering. The evidence of the human condition, I once read, is the ability to work towards a long-term goal. This I know I cannot now do. Have I become inhuman? Am I getting to be Nebuchadnezzar, King of Babylon, one of the few Bible-related persons with whom my father was familiar, who was condemned to eat grass like the cattle of the field and, as my father's memory of the nonsense verses they intoned as children in Jamaica says, "spread his bed in a sardine can"? I pull forward my memory to console myself and to convince myself that even if I have had a stroke and my frontal lobe is gone and with it my claim to be above my Neanderthal forebears, I was once a thinker.

New to Jamaica's slums and only twenty, I was one of those few chosen to do this piece of field research. I was bright then. We were to survey household heads in a depressed part of town. We not only had to be bright; we had to be wise. We were advised that as fieldworkers we should have no emotions. Having emotions and, worse, displaying them while in the field was a methodological sin. I was a bad scientist; I broke the law; I sinned. Approaching a clearing, I saw a little structure no more than five feet by five feet. It had a covering and was wattled up to about a quarter of its height. In it was this six-foot-tall man with his head leaning on one side of the structure and his feet stretched diagonally to the other side. Was this man building a house in which he couldn't even fit? I saw this as funny and had to break the laws of science and laugh. I was in dangerous territory; I was a foreign student and had no large network of locals to protect me: he could be a gunman. How could I laugh at a gunman? I was breaking the laws not only of science but also of survival and wisdom. He empathized: "Laugh, sister, laugh," he said, "for the situation really ridiculous." Had to ask him my raft of questions: Was that where he lived? *Yes.* Was he the head of that household? *Yes. He was.* So the little house was a household. Items and their cost. I was not blind: I could see that he had nothing in it. No chair, no table, no bed, no sofa, no knife, no fork, nor spoon. He and I played the game of completing the questionnaire. It was his time to laugh as he showed me the only thing that he owned: a plastic bottle of tablets. He hadn't even bought this, for he had no money. He had gone downtown to relatives who were well enough off, being proprietors of a drugstore, told them he was ill and had scrounged this bottle of tablets from these relatives who were ashamed of their connection to him and eager to get rid of him. What were the tablets for? *Constipation.* "You see, sister," he offered, "mi don't even have that to put out." He delicately avoided the four-letter word. That is me now. I am and have nothing.

The phone rings and I rush to answer it. Might be someone telling me something that could stimulate. I reach it too late and there is only a dial tone to greet me. Nothing. A car passes by slowly. It is burdened down like a baby with poo in his diaper. It is burdened with sound. Some dancehall rendition which sounds like a tug-of-war between voice and instruments, between throat and nose, between lyrics and music. A dead heat. No one is winning. Stalemate. I am in a sea of nothingness. Is this like "wandering lonely as a cloud"? No. After that wandering came a "host of golden daffodils" and mental stimulation for the poet. What do I see before me as my mind wanders? I see the trumpet tree, that tree whose behaviour informs us about the journey of a hurricane. Its leaves are doing a little shake and wave, the action as taut and controlled as the dancehall rendition. It reminds me of the eye of the storm. No action. The flat phase of the hurricane. Stasis. I see a faded yellow leaf attached to a group of healthy green leaves by a string. The yellow leaf spins in the breeze but it won't fall because it is tethered to a spider's web and cushioned by the green leaves which are still secure on a stem. This ballerina is secure. I remember Conut. What I saw I still cannot and have not put into words. But me? I can put me into words, but wherever are they? Words describe something and I am no thing. They have abandoned me who was once a wordsmith. "Lovely prose," they used to say. I feel like the Arizona of the Zane Grey novels: swaths of light brown sand; no cowboy on the horizon and not even one buffalo or Indian footprint. Nothing is happening. Nothing. Not attached. Not even a dream in my heart.

I have a wish, though. I wish I could see a boy with a kite. He would send the kite up and keep the stick of cord in his hand. He would be looking up anxiously to guide the kite past the electric wires and the tree limbs. I can see him jerk it, and in this gentle wind, I see it going higher and higher. It would be alone in the sky but it would be rooted in the boy's hands. Do

I need religion? Cousin Nothing had been singing or trying to sing some religious thing about "anchor" the first day I met her. I didn't catch all the words: *"I have an anchor" something something,* then, *"Will your anchor hold in the storms of life? We have an anchor."* Do I need an anchor? I remember this line because my grandmother joined her. She had talked too about heaven and the rapture and joining her master in the sky.

I grew up in England and was on my last days of sixth form. I had one paper left to be done. I had opted to do a long paper rather than sit a formal exam and had the summer in which to complete it. We were given a choice of topics – Margaret Mead's contribution to the study of the family, headless tribes in East Africa, or the West Indian family. With roots in the West Indies, I thought this last was tailor-made for me. All I had to do was get family trees from my parents. My father, always eager to help me with my work, was ready. We were going to use our own family as the base for my research and would look at its structure. His first. I assumed we would get to hers later. We set to work, drawing lines and arrows between them. Too often I would hear him say, "Then where does X fit in?"

My mother, more in jest than assistance, once called out, "You first of all have to admit that yours is the 'alternative family'; you are going to fit neatly into no mould. Where are you going to put Conut, your mother's sister who isn't your mother's sister?" We persevered. Then a nice thought hit my father.

"Why don't you go down and spend some time with your grandparents and check out these names. They are in their late eighties by now – how time flies! – but still very bright, I can see from their letters. Just the right time to be visiting old people."

My mother did not think that identifying these people would help my paper. "They would have to be born again and in some order," she said, but added that it would be good for me to go down there.

Like my father, I had attacks of asthma and I think my mother was thinking that a little time out of the London air might clear my bronchials. That's how I came to be with my grandparents visiting Cousin Nothing and hearing her sing about her anchor. My grandparents had looked knowingly at each other when she talked about heaven and the sky. Guess they were congratulating themselves on coming in time.

This lady had the habit of falling down, "dropping down", they called it. Seems she had high blood pressure, and having no blood kin around, my grandparents, her closest relatives as far as the village people knew, would be sent for on these occasions. The telegram had come: "Conut drop down. Come at once." My grandfather obediently hired the only car in the village and we set out for Cousin Nothing's abode. It was not that the old lady looked sick; she just looked vulnerable, and I had assumed that my grandparents would take her home with them for there was ample space there. This was not to be. Seems this was something proposed from time to time and vetoed by the self-same Nothing. My grandfather did the next best thing. He sent for somebody from the village who would stay with her and see to her personal needs.

I could see from their faces that this was not a new suggestion, and the helper would before long be sent on her way for the old lady would declare herself able to see to herself. I am adventurous but I am not the type to take care of my own domestic needs, let alone someone else, and in the deep rural at that, so my offer to stay with Cousin Nothing came when I was certain that a helper would be employed. From their nod and smile, I could see that my grandparents approved of this. I think they were mindful of my project and felt that for my father Herbert's sake they had to expose me to as much information as was there for me to get. The lady helper would look after both of us and get a bit more money than she would have for seeing to Cousin Nothing alone. The lady helper, of course, did not mind. I had heard in the discussions in the car coming down that Conut was a lady who would, as soon as you turned your back, fire the helper but pay her to pretend that she was still working. I suspected that my grandparents felt that with me there, the old lady would have to keep the helper. I stayed with Cousin Nothing.

I had brought no clothes but that was no problem. From the time I reached that village and started going up Nothing's hill, I was hearing those who came out to stare at us and enjoy the drama of Cousin Nothing's "drop down" saying, "What a way she look like Conut. Same fine body." Conut had a wardrobe full of clothes she was yet to wear, clothes that were in style – I should say, had come back in style – that could fit me. My underwear I was prepared to wash nightly and partially dry in a towel. I had learnt this in camp. Having towel-dried them, I could put them behind the fridge –

Cousin Nothing had one – and have clean dry underwear for the morning. In any case, there was what they called a "dry goods" store only two miles away where it seemed I could get all sort of things. I had money. Did I have the capacity to walk two miles? I imagined my underwear recycled to infinity, or whenever they came back for me.

Cousin Nothing had not looked like I thought death should look. Her eyes were still bright and shining, and though her feet were thin like matchsticks, they were far from dead. She was marching them as she sat, to the sound of her song. She was remembering "Christian Endeavour Days", she said, clearly enough for my grandmother to hear and nod in assent and of course for me, who didn't have any referent for that term, to remember the words. Seems to me she would be able to answer my questions and help me with my paper. I was coming to distrust my grandparents' answers. I think I was getting the sanitized version of things, even beginning to feel that certain people were to be left out of the family tree. The comment "Where Herbert find these names to give you?" I read to mean *We kept Herbert away from knowing those people, how come he still got to know them to be his relatives?* Perhaps if I had not been there for the telegram about Conut, I would not have been invited to go with them and would not have met this cousin of mine about whom my mother teased my father and who was the responsibility of these two old people, my grandmother and grandfather.

Seeing things in the sky which nobody else sees is not new to me. One time after my return to England, I saw very clearly the big wooden bowl like a saucer in which I had bathed in that important fortnight when I stayed with Cousin Nothing. Now in my feeling of nothingness, I look in the skies and there is Cousin Nothing like Mary Poppins floating in the skies on her sisal mat, anchored by the skein of cord in the boy's hand. I know that the Dead Sea feeling will pass, for I now feel I have a purpose: to write about Cousin Nothing. Not as I did in that paper a million years ago when I was finishing sixth form, but to complete her circles, pulling the straw back, then forward, and stitching it onto the layer before. You should have seen that mat and its evolution! What was unfolding before our eyes as we worked was amazing. It was all things bright and beautiful, and we were making it.

Some people remember their honeymoon. My two-week stay with Cousin Nothing is of that order. Most memorable, and I would like to say transforming, though I have yet to find the courage to allow myself to be really transformed. I liked her. As they say here, "My spirit take her." Her spirit must have taken me too, for her eyes followed me as I moved from the little back veranda on which she sat with my grandparents, to the brick oven that took up all of the kitchen, to the oil house, to the cane mill. She fell completely in love with me when I asked for a machete, cut my first root of cane and peeled it with the machete, a thing I had only heard could be done.

To this day I cannot figure out whether Conut's "dropping down", which had brought my grandparents to her deathbed time and time again, was a hoax or not, for with them gone, Conut put on her water boots and set out, like I imagined old plantation owners of yesteryear did, to walk around her farm, with me behind her pee-pee cluck-cluck. With each step she got stronger. "Man cannot live without plants," she constantly mumbled. Coming from London, I of course thought of it the other way around: "Plants cannot live without man." Our house had millions of plants but they were like babies, having to be sat when we went off on our annual two-week holiday to the beach, by an official plant keeper who was paid to give them water, and the orchids, their special orchid food. The rhododendrum had to have their leaves dusted and cleaned like a young baby, so that they could be shiny, and the roses had to have their spent blooms picked off.

"You are going to like this place." "We are going to be friends." These were the only words that passed between us as we walked, and they came from Cousin Nothing. I answered nothing, not a word. Hunger forced speech out of me. I was smelling Miss Cookie's hand, so I suggested that we go back to the house. The table was set and the food was piping hot. Seated at the table, Cousin Nothing prayed. This was no longer strange, for my grandparents did that too. I was ready to dig in when she pulled the plate with the chicken from me. "Does your father eat the flesh of chickens?" she asked. My answer was "Yes, he does but for some reason doesn't think he should." Beneath my answer, I could hear my mother's voice, for this was one of their battle pieces: "This is not red meat. It is the most innocuous of flesh foods. It will do you good. Another foolishness your family sent you out in the world with." The interview continued: "Does your grandmother eat it?" The answer was "No." "Why do they have this negative approach to the eating of the flesh of fowls?" I knew the answer to that, having asked it a thousand times at home. My father didn't enjoy chicken for he was brought up to think of it as "dirty meat". "And your grandmother? Did you ask her?" I had, but she had only said that fowls were nasty things; they ate lizards and centipedes and all sorts of ugly things which they scratched from garbage dumps. "But," I wondered to her as my mother had wondered aloud to my father on several occasions, "that was domestically grown chickens. The chickens served on tables in this day and age do not run wild and therefore do not eat nasty things; they are in coops and are fed corn." I could say this confidently and see my mother's point, for I had been on a field trip to a chicken factory. I was hardly finished with my answer before Cousin Nothing moved into her informative speech and poor me, having no tape recorder with me at that point to record it!

She talked about how my grandmother had come back from Panama sick to death from one of those fevers they seem to manufacture there. One day she got so sick that Cousin Nothing and Cousin Nothing's mother or adopted mother, or whatever, were discussing what they would bury her in and where. Then suddenly they heard a commotion in the yard and saw a conference of the fowls. A hen flew up, higher than she had ever seen one fly, and dropped heavily to the ground, dead. On what they had thought would any minute be a deathbed, there was a shuffling, then feet dragging on the floor; it was my grandmother holding tentatively to the wall and coming out to see what all the noise was about. It was she who said, "Give thanks," asked for some vegetable soup and sat in the rocking chair, while Nothing and her mother stared in disbelief. Apparently grandmother was healed from that moment. And of course was more resolved than ever never to eat chicken's flesh from that day on.

Nothing explained to me what I think is called a "sympathetic relationship": my grandmother and the fowls were in a sympathetic and dependent relationship – "symbiotic", I think the word is. All things have their duty on earth but all things sometimes face tragedy and cannot do their work. My grandmother, though she didn't know it all along, was aware that chickens had their work to do, Nothing informed me. Calling them nasty was just a rationalization which kept my grandmother, from childhood, a non-eater of the flesh of fowls. The chicken gave its life to save my grandmother for it knew that she had work that only she could do; my grandmother in return continued to respect and protect chickens and their cleaning tasks even more from that day, and felt within herself that she must fight to allow them to do this. To kill and eat a chicken is to keep it from cleaning the earth. My grandmother knew this, Nothing said; has known this in some way or another from childhood and that is why she does not eat the flesh of fowls and that is "why your grandmother fostered a negative attitude towards the eating of the flesh of fowls in your father as a child", she made me know.

My grandmother's match in the animal world was the fowl and they both knew that they were each other's guardian in this world of sin and woe, Nothing continued with her lecture. "Don't eat this chicken child and your father shouldn't be eating it either," she strongly advised. "Your family has the task of keeping this cleaner cleaning the earth. Your children shouldn't eat it either. This is a world of corruption. Everybody and everything needs a little protection," she ended and called Miss Cookie to prepare some vegetables with cheese for me. I noticed that she was making headway with the plate of chicken, and asked why. She pushed a plate before me. "This is dasheen. You may eat this. I cannot." I asked no more questions. I realized then that my grandmother and Cousin Nothing were not as close kin as I had thought. Nothing did not stop there. For reasons which I was to understand not much later, she called Cookie and asked her to bring a dasheen for me to see and feel. She brought one clean and one dirty. I duly saw and felt and asked questions to which I got answers: "Yes. It comes out of the earth. That one has been cleaned; the other has not been."

The next day we walked again, "ran the farm", I think it is called. This was after breakfast so I didn't have the desire to go back home from this walk prematurely to eat. We walked as far as a little bamboo house with thatched roof. Nothing did not knock or call out; she simply pushed the door and what I saw challenged me to revise the notions of evolution I had learnt at school. I saw Keith, a large version of a dasheen. He was sitting in the corner on the dirt floor. This dasheen had not been cleaned of the dirt from which it had come: that he was sitting on the earthen floor with his hands around his knees and that he was pigeon-chested made the image more stark, for the human features – the hands and the feet – were disguised and all you could see was a blob, a big blob, a big ball, earth-toned and hairy like the dasheen which has just been dug from the earth. He tried to speak and his tongue escaped – a bluish thing, the dead stamp of the thing I had eaten the night before. Nothing went over and tilted him. His eyes opened but this made very little difference to his non-human look, for they were just slits mirroring the ringed marks of the dasheen, an illusion firmly supported by the so-called shirt he was wearing. It was earth-toned, from dirt, I think, but originally must have had stripes running horizontally, like the indentations in a dasheen.

I knew a story was coming and that I would have to listen carefully, for again, I did not have my tape recorder with me and, more important, neither my grandparents nor my father, I was sure, knew this story. I doubt whether they knew of Keith's existence. I was sure that even if they did know, they would not have shared their knowledge with me. Nothing didn't even bother to wait until we were outside. She started right there with Keith listening. "But first," she said, "the pleasant part. Sing for her, Keith." Out of this dasheen came the sweetest sounds. I felt like Wordsworth listening to the solitary reaper. Even as he sang, Nothing spoke.

"Miss Aileen sent to call me. This is not a today thing," she advised me. Just as well, for I knew not who Miss Aileen was. "She was on her deathbed and wanted to confess. She and her mate had been stealing my father's dasheens. I had heard the story of this new tuber which only my father had successfully planted in commercial quantities; how it fetched high prices on the market, but my father could not get to reap them and make the profit due to him. She said that he had given warning: "When oonoo see oonoo pickney come out looking like dasheen, a dat time oonoo a go know sey oonoo fi stop tief mi dasheen but it a go too late." She didn't know whether she was just red-eyed and tiefing because the things were there, or whether it was a craving, something over which she had no control, something her body desperately needed, driving her. Her young man thought it was a craving, given her state of pregnancy, something the baby needed and he would continue going to the dasheen patch even when she had stopped going. Then he stopped but her body kept craving after dasheen. She must have bathed after one intense hankering, and the baby in her stomach at an impressionable age caught her sentiment as she dried her body all over. She didn't know whether my father knew that she was the one stealing them, or whether somebody had put a hex on her and her man and forced them to steal, but the result was a dasheen baby.

She had to keep him secret and locked away for she didn't want people to know that prophecy had been fulfilled on her. Moreover, if they saw the child they would certainly have declared that she had brought the devil into their midst, and been tempted to chop it up and feed it to hogs like you did young banana. The father didn't want to have anything to do with her or the child. He wanted to have more children but said he couldn't trust her body to produce a real child. Even if he could stomach this one, who is to say that in another pregnancy she wouldn't crave after green banana and bring a child with toes and fingers like a hand of banana, so she was alone with Keith.

It was my father, she said, who helped her out. He gave her a square of land which she worked for herself and on it he helped her to build a little house in the bush to which Keith and herself moved out of the public gaze. He was a good child, she said, and knew to keep away from people. All they could ever hear was the singing, and since she could sing well too, she could join him and people never bothered to think who was the other being living with her. "What was I to do?" Nothing was not really asking me. Just talking to the wind. "My father must have poisoned some of the dasheens out of sheer frustration and she, poor woman or her poor mate, dug the ones that he had so doctored. After a hurricane had battered their little house, I built what I told people would be a storehouse and I put Keith in it. His mother died, but me, now I can't die, for who will take Keith?"

Cousin Nothing had a dilemma. I could see why she couldn't eat dasheens; I could also feel her guilt at what her father had caused. When we exited Keith's house she said something more. "About this time my mother died. She was diagnosed by the doctors as suffering from tuberculosis but the people here say that she got quite yellow before she died. That only happens when you have been poisoned, they said, and Miss Aileen's passed-over people must have come back and taken revenge for what my father did. They even say that their revenge was meant for me but my mother took the blow." I didn't totally understand what I was told but I could empathize with her. What a secret to be keeping hidden in her outhouse! What a burden! She was crying. No sound coming from her. Just the tears that I couldn't help but see. Should such an old woman be crying? I don't know that I had ever seen a person over forty crying. Anyhow, I asked what I had to ask: "Is he my relative by blood?" "Anything can happen," she said, and I was reminded of my mother.

Conut did not call me to keep her company the next day but she did the day after. "So you want to know your family line."

"Yes," I said and went for my diagram.

She glanced at it, put it on the table, and said, "Come."

We walked down to the outhouse with our cutlasses. The thought struck me that we were going to cut Keith and see whether he had my blood in his veins. Keith came out with his cutlass and we went farther into the bush. We stopped at a very attractive but frightening plant. Reminded me of the triffids. It had multiple arms, rising stiff from its stalk like those of a ballet dancer. They said it was the ping wing macca, and I was glad to meet this plant about which my father sometimes sang: "*Mi heng it pon ping wing macca.*" Its edges were serrated like a saw. Why would anybody want to hang a dress on ping wing macca?

Conut intervened into my thoughts to inform me that some plants were particularly good. We could know them by the fact that their growth progression followed the natural path. And what was this natural path? One leaf would emerge, then another, then two – the sum of one and one – then three – the sum of two and one, then five would merge – the sum of two and three, then eight – the sum of five and three, and so on, the number of leaves continuing to determine the next number of leaves to infinity. Just as there was a law of creativity laid down by the Supreme Being who did his work then saw that it was good before going on to another task, so there was a natural process of growth and it was that we should always double back to base before going forward. I was never good at botany so this lecture was not for me. What could I do with this bit of information? They say here that if certain people say something, even if it is not so, "it nearly go so". I left Conut's intervention there. The macca plant did observe this law of nature. I assume that I was supposed to see it, despite its prickles, as a good plant.

We chopped this beneficent plant, releasing its various fronds. I was advised to see to it that the juice didn't get on my skin. How could that be accomplished? So as we went home, I was the one itching. Conut was not helpful. "You think you begin to scratch yet? Wait 'til we start to clean it." But when we went home and moved into the process of washing the separated fronds she did give me a long-sleeved plastic garment to put on, and I was able to scrape and cut and wash like everybody else without digging my skin off to relieve itching. We hit this poor plant to pulp with stones, then scraped off all its green with short knives until a stringy interior emerged. We worked until we had a pile of strings called sisal. We washed this and left them hanging from a line. Then we called it a day and I went to my bed, Miss Cookie to her cooking, Keith back to his bamboo outhouse and Conut to wherever she went. But if Miss Cookie was seeing Keith, he could not be a secret, I realized in that half-sleep state. It was the story of Keith rather than the existence of Keith that was the secret. Well, nobody in that village, certainly not Miss Cookie, was going to hear the true story of Keith from me.

All other days, it seemed, would be devoted to using the sisal, which was now dried and coiled. Did I say that we had combed the strings? Combed them to take all the tangles out and twisted the strings into strong cord. It was my time to send a telegram to my grandparents: "Taking one more week. Don't come for me 'til next week Friday." I was caught up in the activity and did not see it ending before the following week. As if to accommodate me, all farm work stopped and Keith, Conut and I, and Miss Cookie from time to time, focused on making what Cousin Nothing told me would be a mat. Strands were taken out and like the emperor's craftsmen in just about any fairy tale, we set to work with small amounts of strands in the left hand which we curled using the first three fingers of that hand, flipping the wrist so that we made circles, then fastening the bunched curled strands at regular intervals with sisal threads from our needles propelled by the right hand.

"Your end is your beginning," Conut advised, so that we knew the initial set of strands had to be long enough to make our circles and leave over to begin the next, which we could then gently and neatly supply with more strands as needed. As we worked, Conut talked about the family. At nights I tried to put the data into the grid I had brought. No can do. I decided to focus on the never-ending circles that we were making that seemed like a mat of family.

2. maud

Out of the blue Miss Maud had bawled out to her charge, "Gal, a breed you a breed? You tink mi nuh see the lizard jump pon you?"

The girl's response was to shake out her dress, for she was mortally afraid of lizards. From that day Miss Maud watched her like a hawk. Nobody had bothered to tell her how old she was, and since birthdays were not things celebrated there, she could not say, *Mary is having her sweet sixteen party. I am the same height as she, so I must be about sixteen too.* What she knew was that she was "out of school". That meant that she was a big young miss. If there was a younger child in the yard she would have a handle put on her name. She would be Sister Clarise or Miss Clarise or even Cousin Clarise. As it was, her guardian rarely called her anything but Gal.

Another day Miss Maud crept up behind her and shouted in her ears, "You ah see you health?" She didn't feel sick so she said, "Yes." It was not the time when people talked about fallopian tubes and eggs in the womb and penises. Nobody had even told her about blood coming at certain times from the same place from which pee came. She had since last Christmas been having the blood as well as pee. She had told no one, for this was not the kind of thing that a decent girl talked about and all girls were decent so there were none to say to her, *This happened to me too.* She had simply put dried banana trash in her step-ins until it stopped. She hadn't needed to do this for some time, which meant to her that she was indeed now seeing her health – no blood was coming. It was at this late stage that the lesson came: "When blood a come out a you cuttie, you healthy. When it nah come, something wrong wid you."

She was really feeling bilious lately and there was no blood, so perhaps she was not healthy, but she wasn't going to tell Miss Maud that, for Miss Maud didn't like sicky-sicky people around her. She called them delicate alabaster baby. She didn't want to be called that ever again. She wanted to be strong like Miss Maud wanted her to be. Neville was her good friend but not even he knew of the blood thing. They played that game where they showed each other their private parts, and even tried to join them after Neville told her that she had a hole there, but she never did that when there was blood. She would just say, "I cannot play today", and he never urged her nor was vexed.

On one occasion when they were playing that game, Mass Eustace, whose land abutted Miss Maud's, jumped the barbwire fence and came over claiming that he was going to tell. They couldn't at first imagine what he was going to tell, for they were not stealing cane or ripe bananas or anything like that and they had not harmed anybody's fowl or goat or anything; they were only sharing what was theirs – their bodies. Whereupon Mass Eustace asked them what they thought Adam and Eve were doing when God chased them out of the Garden of Eden. Before they could tell him that it was an apple that Adam and Eve had stolen and they had stolen none, it wasn't even apple time, he told them it was not an apple, it was what they were doing, and he would tell Pastor who would drive them out of Christian Endeavour.

Christian Endeavour was a big deal. Only well-behaved children were in it. And you wore a special ribbon on your shirt or blouse and marched into the church after all the elders were seated. Pastor would beam from the pulpit and say, "Give the young battalion the way. Let them come in." Nobody wanted to be driven out of that. They wouldn't do it again, they pleaded. Mass Eustace knew a way to stop him from talking: Clarise should link with him this one time and not do it again. Neither she nor Neville saw anything difficult about that, and so Mass Eustace lifted up Clarise and put her legs around his waist, telling Neville to turn his back, which he duly did. It was different from with Neville for a kind of glue was left at the top of her legs which she had to wipe off, and he was now telling her that she should not tell Miss Maud about this. This glue didn't happen with Neville nor did he make up his face and grunt like Mass Eustace was doing.

Everyone kept their word. No one was driven out of Christian Endeavour; Neville and Clarise never tried to link again and of course Miss Maud heard nothing of the affair. Nor did Mass Eustace ask for a repeat. But from that time Clarise never had to use the dried banana trash in her step-ins again.

In those days women were not showing off their breasts and their legs: clothes were worn loose. Clarise had had no occasion to see her whole body – there was no full-length mirror around – or to strip off all her clothes and see herself. One simply tidied the crucial parts with a soaped piece of cloth and a pan of water. She therefore did not see that her breasts were swelling nor that the bottom of her belly was increasing and getting stiff. There was never any need to go to the dressmaker to get measured. Clothes made for her were not a part of Clarise's life. There was a church basket with very nice, almost-new clothes coming in from all parts of the world and definitely in style. More often than not, they were a little bigger than Clarise's real form, if fitting well was important, and it was not, so nothing was really too tight for her. It was when the baby was squirming out of her – a seven-month baby – that she screamed, now in the full knowledge that she was unhealthy.

She was in the latrine and might have pulled out the stuff looking like a young dog that was sticking out of her and thrown it in the latrine hole, if it had not cried and Miss Maud had not forced her way in. Miss Maud asked her what was wrong. Clarise said, "Nothing, mam," for she felt quite all right in her body, just emotionally upset that this thing had come out of her. Miss Maud had a sense of humour and for all her gruffness, tons of humanity. She checked the little thing and said, "So dis ya something wid two legs, ten toes and ten fingers, and a head is 'nothing'. Ah dat you baby name, Gal?" After that, when people said they hadn't seen Clarise in some time, was something wrong, Miss Maud said, "Nothing wrong."

In those days women didn't go down the street pushing their bellies and with their navels sticking out like the lid of a pot. People didn't go around announcing the birth of a child unless the union between the parents had been blessed by God in the church. In this case, a blessing would be very long in coming, for Clarise couldn't, and, Miss Maud thought, *wouldn't* even reveal the name of the person who had put the seed in her womb, so a marriage was totally impossible. If Miss Maud were of a different class, she would have found discreet transportation to take Nothing and her mother out of the district and to her mother, an aunt or whoever, but she wasn't, so people couldn't avoid hearing a baby cry and couldn't help but know that a baby existed. When they asked questions. Was Clarise all right? Or even, What was making that noise? – Miss Maud said, "Nothing," leading people to make comments like "Nothing over Miss Maud a bawl," "Hear Nothing deh ah bawl."

It was Parson who forced himself into the house, ostensibly to find out why Clarise was not at Christian Endeavour. It was he who described linking to her and asked her with whom she had linked. Neville's name came up and so did Mass Eustace's. Parson preferred Mass Eustace. Neville was a little boy not even out of school as yet and had got a half scholarship to a little-known private school, but high school nonetheless. His parents were solid members of the church. Parson didn't want to spoil his future nor the reputation of his family. He wasn't even asked about his role in the linking. It was Mass Eustace whom Parson confronted. Yes. There had been that link but it had only been on one occasion, just one, so it could not be his seed that had borne fruit. They could give the baby his name but they would get nothing from him. Nothing. Miss Maud wouldn't take the name, so the baby took her and Clarise's last name, Walker, a name she had given them when they came into the village. Miss Maud, Clarise and the baby were the big joke in the village. Naturally the name Nothing stuck to her even though she had a birth paper which said "June".

The seed was a circular mat about the size of a side plate. In my mind I called this Miss Maud. Smaller ones in descending order were crafted and I gave them names.

3. mass eustace

Before Nothing, Mass Eustace had not chick, child nor wife. His link with Clarise was one in a blue moon. Whatever else had come to him of that kind had done so in a similar way – some woman taking pity on him for a single occasion. It was not a situation he thought healthy. The Bible ordered man to increase and multiply. It also said it was better to marry than to burn, and that a man should leave his parents and cleave unto his wife. His life was not healthy at all. And now the little pickney and her mother had his name all over the place. If nothing had happened with the other women, why would it happen with this girl-child who wasn't even righted? Even Parson was telling lies on him. Just like the district people. All kind of lies about him and his cows, lies that even stopped him from getting men to come in and work for him. Jealous. He had come in and done what those living there for generations had not done. He had built a nice two-bedroom house with veranda and had a sturdy kitchen and latrine, none of them thatched business. He had seven well-planted acres of land and three still in ruinate waiting to be cleared and cultivated. What he needed now was a good companion, a lady, but it was like the village had set out to starve him. No decent woman was staring back at him when his eyes caught one; none sent a pudding for him or offered to mend his clothes.

Now and again he saw the little baby. It was now looking more like a baby. That thing which they had shown him and which he did have to reject had looked like a little puppy dog in a whole heap of cloth. Sometimes he would see Clarise and the baby nearby the line. There were orange trees and guava trees growing in the line. As such they could be picked by anyone – he or Miss Maud. For years those trees had been a problem between them, for Miss Maud had behaved as if they were hers and it was a struggle for him to get any of the fruit. If he talked to her about it, he would hear that he had enough – what were two oranges and two guavas which he didn't even have enough mouths to eat? It was the principle of the thing. It should be share and share alike. These days he found himself picking from the high branches which they couldn't reach and giving to what was really two pickney. Strange though, when he looked in the baby's face, he would see his mother and a sadness would come over him. All the hard work of building house and buying land had been for her and just when he was able to buy her the only two things she had ever asked for – a reading glass and a bureau with a looking glass – she died.

There was a root of cane that had taken to travelling from his plot and sitting itself right in the line. He told Clarise that that was hers and the baby's and he would even cut and peel cane for them. He found himself caring, biting up the cane in his own mouth and then giving it to the baby, for he knew she hadn't firm enough teeth to master the peeling and chewing.

When his sister Euphemia came to visit from Panama, she heard the story about the fathering of Nothing and took herself over to Miss Maud to see and pronounce on the child. There she found her mother's nose upon the child. She remonstrated with her brother: "You don't even have a puss kitten. You want people fi keep on a sey you de wid man and with animal. Tek the girl. She no too sensible but she must can cook and even if she can't cook, she must can tidy up and raise the baby. You soon fifty. You nah get no younger. You soon ah go need somebody fi turn you when you get bed sore. You ah mi twin and me would love fi come turn you but mi and you are the same age. The two of wi old. Me nah go able look after you. And look where mi live! Tek the baby and raise her as you daughter. You can't lose out off of that."

When she went back, she sent lots of pretty clothes made in America for the baby. Sometimes she even sent the parcel through him and Mass Eustace had to carry it over to Miss Maud, who would behave like Mass

Eustace had thought up the gift and was taking it to the baby personally. She would put the baby on his knees and in his arms and tell her that her father had brought something for her. The baby liked the feel of a man's strong muscles and Mass Eustace got to like playing with his miniature mother.

Things were moving towards a natural transfer of Nothing and her mother to Mass Eustace's house, when the consumption took Clarise and the sanitary inspector said that mother and child had to be separated. Miss Maud didn't ask any questions. She knew that this was a bad "sick" and if they did not comply within three days, the officer would come back with a black van and cart them all off to a kind of prison made specially for people with that sickness. She just took Nothing over to Mass Eustace and she herself stayed with the baby for the first few days. This way only Clarise would be taken away.

Miss Maud had no tears to shed over this matter and shed none. The truth is that she had been beginning to feel mother things. Since the maroon man and his friends mash up her front after the autoclaps in Morant Bay, Miss Maud was sure she didn't want to have anything to do with those things. She knew that meant that she wouldn't have any children. Her little sister would have to be her child, and she was. She watched Clarise breast-feeding Nothing and she didn't think she would like having something sucking her like she was a sow pig, but what she did envy was Nothing's demand for her mother's breast. She would have liked some little person to climb on her lap and put her hand in her blouse and take out her breast. Not the sucking. The sense of the need to connect with her was what she wanted to feel. Nothing didn't do that with her. In fact she and Nothing could be quite cuddly together and it would be as if Nothing smelt her mother's milk and she would start struggling to get to Clarise.

That wouldn't last forever. Nothing, like all babies, would have to be weaned and this came relatively easily and quickly, for Clarise was one of those women whose milk didn't stay around long. "Gal, you have fi start cook special pot fi di baby." It was Miss Maud, though, who cooked for the baby, who blew her porridge with her breath to get it cold enough for her; it was she who lifted her up and spoon-fed her. Soon it was to her that Nothing went for food and affection. Clarise didn't try to compete. She said nothing when Miss Maud taught Nothing to call her "Mama", while she called her Clarise, who had given birth to the child, Ga-Ga, her version of the "Gal" that Miss Maud continued to call her. She just stayed in the back, general factotum to Nothing and Miss Maud. Then the consumption took them both away from her and left her with her sick self as company.

Some premature babies grow to be fat babies and fat children. At five when Nothing went over to Mass Eustace she was still a little wisp of a body. Mass Eustace would swing her up to his shoulder or onto his back for jockey ride and say, "Little girl, you are as light as a feather. No wonder they call you 'Nothing'." Nothing grew up believing that it was because she was small that they called her Nothing. Mass Eustace did not say of her "this is mine" until she reached seven and was going out to elementary school. Those days they didn't ask for birth certificates: Mass Eustace just said to the head teacher who already knew him, "I have come to register June." And the teacher, who knew all the village business, didn't bother to ask his relationship with her. She just put him down as father, asking him only if Eustace Reid was his right name. Nothing went down into the education side of government as June Reid, while in the Spanish Town side where all the age papers are kept, she was June Walker, and of course Nothing to everybody else. It would have been stupid for Mass Eustace to do anything else but own her, for even if he was not June's real father she certainly was now his adopted daughter and even stepdaughter, for with Clarise gone, Miss Maud was acting like she was June's mother and Miss Maud was so much over at Mass Eustace now that people thought of them as a couple.

Mass Eustace had seen many pictures of bride and groom. There was even a framed picture of his mother and his father after their church wedding. The man was always at least a head above the woman. Miss Maud was a big strapping woman; he reached her at her neck. He didn't think they made a good couple but Miss Maud was acting otherwise. She didn't fully move in, and she had got Lily to come in and look after him and the baby. Lily was smaller, more like the bride in the pictures, but Miss Maud had no intention of letting Lily and her size become any bride to Mass Eustace. She settled her in the extra room, which was Nothing's room, and made it clear that she was to sleep with Nothing. When Miss Maud came over, she made a big thing of spending a long time in Mass Eustace room. Only she was to tidy it and to sleep in it.

Meanwhile she got Mass Eustace to understand that she had feelings. She might be older than he, though she doubted it and even then, that didn't say.

And if he was looking for a woman whom no man could whisper about, he had found one. She told him about the maroon man and other little secrets like that and he told her about his lack of success with women, whereupon Miss Maud told him that he could stop talking about that now, for he was successful with her. It took some time for her to get over the memory and the fear that the maroon man had left her with but she did, and Mass Eustace in his old age began to sample on a regular basis and in an assigned space that which was offered to men who did not care to burn. Nothing now had a real family. More than that she now not only had a cane root but several coconut trees, for every birthday Mass Eustace planted another coconut tree for her. The returns from whatever coconuts, dried or jelly, were sold from those trees went into an account at the post office for Nothing.

By the time I met Cousin Nothing she had given up the Walker and Reid and was now Tull, the name of a second husband. Had I met her ten years before she would have been officially June Turnbury. Last names she could give up but nobody allowed her to give up her pet name. She continued to be a slim, little thing. You could blow her down with one breath. It was easier, they said, to blow her down than to blow wood fire into flames. At school everyone lifted her and said how she was light and it was just as well that she was called "Nothing". It was the delight of the courting males to lift her up and run with her. "You are as light as a feather. I can see why they call you Nothing." Miss Maud never forgot why she was called Nothing and she had given Mass Eustace the story. I doubt that Cousin Nothing knew it. My grandmother learnt it from Mass Eustace's sister, my grand-aunt or great-grand-aunt – does kinship terminology matter? – the one in Panama who continued to send things for Nothing, including a wedding dress that the village talked about for ages. That was the first wedding. That one began a very short marriage, the one to Turnbury.

4. everard turnbury

Everard Turnbury came off of a good table. Surprisingly it was his father, a thorough white man, who spoilt up things. Mother had been a Smith, dark but that didn't too much matter for she was the daughter of Captain Smith, a stipendiary magistrate who had come from the British Isles. Unlike his peers who had taken women from the ex-slave population and not legitimized their relationships, Captain Smith had. None of the stipendiary magistrates were young men but they didn't seem to realize that. Captain Smith was one of the few among them blessed with this intelligence and therefore knew that at fifty-plus, new to the tropics, death would not be far away. He took the opportunity of a government job with a monthly salary to buy himself a nice farm and build himself a nice house in which to leave his black wife and their mulatto children.

It was Doris Smith's own father, Captain Smith, who had made the match and lived to regret it, for his wife had nursed him successfully through the pneumonia which he had expected to take him off at seventy, man's allotted age, as written in the Bible. He had hurried up to give Doris away to Samuel Turnbury in a respectable ceremony. Samuel was the son of Turnbury, who had a little estate nearby and only one son to inherit it. Captain Smith had argued to himself that with what Doris would get from him at his death and with the Turnbury estate, she could continue his care of the other four children and perhaps help them to professions.

You had to make your girl-children secure especially if they had a tip of African blood in them, for men of all stripes tended to believe that they were easy pickings. Most of the mulatto women he knew were tough like men and ran bawdy houses in which they kept their own sisters in virtual slavery. The less tough ones were just concubines. The thought of his Doris in one of these tragic positions brought tears to his eyes. He had seen young Turnbury eyeing her. He imagined that with his own death, one such as he would take the opportunity to turn her into the tragic mulatto. To prevent this, he formally offered marriage. He knew that the Turnbury estate was in deep financial troubles, the main problem being the lack of hard cash to replace machinery. He gave them an offer they could not refuse: hard cash to buy machinery went with Doris. He lived long enough to see his money spent on horses and the young fool didn't even have the good sense to buy one of the horses he was betting on and pay himself from time to time. All Doris's dowry went like salt physic through the body to the owners of the British Horse Market nearby. Captain Smith hoped that the fellow knew shame and that the drinking was some sign of this, for as he lost the money to horses, so he drank, and rum was such an easy thing to get on his or any of the many estates around.

The fellow had a good side. He was sweet and giving when he was drunk. He would turn out his pockets and give the last cent to anyone who asked for it. No wonder he could always get rum even if it was the last bottle needed to complete some order to send to the shippers. Doris didn't worry her head too much or complain, for he was nicer to her when he was drunk than when he was sober. It was this niceness that helped them to fill their quiver, to have out Doris's lot as the Bible said was right. The children were made in pickled seminal fluid which Doris could only get to flow when the donor was corned. The family was unusual.

Captain Smith went when Doris came to visit with the fourth pregnancy, walking in the house without slippers and trying to tell him that shoes kept her feet too confined; she didn't mind freeing them up while she was inside. His daughter walking barefooted! Feet that had always been in blue or pink slippers lined with the fur of some animal. No mind it is in the house. Doris walking barefooted! She went on to make two more while her husband drank the Turnbury estate away and the cash which she had brought into the marriage. Her brothers had managed to be professional, lawyers, teachers and accountants. Her children had no hope of being anything like that. How much was colour worth without financial backative? If Everard had not been so down and out he would not have been available to June and been part of Conut's and my story.

Mass Eustace was somehow related to me. It took me some time to work out how. The family came from Hanover. They did not have colour; they did not have professions; they did not have lands. All they had was the willingness to work and to move and keep on moving. They were neither afraid of work nor belligerent. It was these kinds of people who got lands to buy when the estates were willing to sell out some of their back lands. They had formed a gang of brothers and sisters and had come to Clarendon and worked on the estate as a unit. They paid down on the land as a group, worked it as a group and were able to pay for it before the time contracted and were now free to find other jobs. Some had the money to go to Cuba; some had money to set up a little shoemaking business in Panama. Mass Eustace went nowhere. His movement was within Jamaica. He settled in neighbouring St Ann, selling out his Clarendon holding and buying ten nice green acres. He was old when he reached St Ann. Nearly fifty when he linked with Clarise and nearly sixty when Miss Maud forced her big self on him and made him part of the community. Miss Maud had her own farm to manage; Nothing was too skinny to do much work with the hoe; her little hands could not even circle the handle. She was not made for bush work, Mass Eustace said, and had a dressmaker come and teach her how to sew, embroider and do other craft work. Lily's business was keeping house and he wanted her to continue keeping the house, for without a good house, Nothing would not get a good man.

It was at this point that Everard came into his life, came too into the circle of mats. Brown pointed-nose Everard asked him for work. Banana was coming in. Everyone said that this was where money was. Mass Eustace gave Everard the three acres still in ruinate to turn into bananas and the man turned them into gold. It was not so much the ability to make the banana grow; it was his ability to get it sold. Everard knew the big men, they being of his colour and table and a class he would have been in if his father had not messed up. He also had his eye on the prize. The old man was going; he had no heir but the girl. The farm and the banana business could come to him if he played his cards right. He got Mass Eustace to buy himself a mule and cart to take the bananas to the wharf. Then he told him not to pay him for his labour with money from his pocket, instead to give him the mule and cart and allow him to pay off for it with labour.

The transportation of the bananas was now Everard's business. He managed to get others to move into banana cultivation and to have him take their bananas to the wharf. People were getting what looked like gold for this lowly plant which you had to pretend you were only cooking to feed your pigs, not to put in your plate. People were now buying all sorts of heavy things with their banana money. Teacher bought an organ; Mr Gillies bought a cane mill; Mr Cullington was regularly buying rice and cloth and lamps in large quantities to set up what he called a haberdashery. All this transporting was done by Everard, and his banana-buying friends showed him how to buy and drive a truck. His business was bursting at the seams and, though it did not look like it, he knew that Mass Eustace was really the base of it, for he had no land he would call his own and had to depend on what Mass Eustace allowed him to work.

Mass Eustace conveniently died, so conveniently that questions were asked. His donkey had run away with him and man and donkey were found days later in a wooded area to which the searchers were guided by circling crows. The donkey had got tied up in withes and had slipped, throwing Mass Eustace on to a stone which damaged his skull and brain. This was not a normal death. People could see the hand of man in this. Donkeys are patient beings. They know that the world "no level" and particularly the part of it that they find themselves in, but they are prepared to accept their lot. That donkey had been with Mass Eustace for more than ten years. It knew where Mass Eustace wanted to go more than Mass Eustace himself. Why would the donkey ups and run away with him to a place that neither of them knew? It had something to do with the truck and the truck belonged to the whitish man who felt he was better than the whole of them and was craving after Mass Eustace land – for what is truck? It can break down anytime but land can't done.

Everard moved from the little house he had built near to the three acres of banana, into Mass Eustace's house, where he slept in the sitting room. He gave out that the farm, the whole farm, needed him. Nobody could deny that about the bananas for nobody was as good at growing bananas as Everard. Nobody knew the banana business as well as he. But the dasheen and coconuts and so on? No. They were doing quite well before he came on. Then he gave out that it looked bad for a young man and a young woman to be living in a house and not married, no mind he was camping in the living room and not in Nothing's room. Miss Maud was not sorry that he was saying that for he had taken to looking at Nothing in a way she did not like. When he suggested marriage, she agreed.

Perhaps Everard did not know about Mass Eustace's sister in Panama. She came home and raised hell, though she had liked the idea of marriage and had actually sent Nothing the wedding dress. The hell started by letter. She had written to Miss Maud to ask who had killed her brother. This concreted the idea in Miss Maud's head that the death was not normal. When the sister came home, they knocked heads together and, deciding that the brown man had done something to Eustace or to his donkey, they set out to see that what he hoped to get he would not get. If they could help it he was not going to get Mass Eustace land through marriage or any other way.

Things played into their hands: he hit the girl and more, carried their business outside. Everard knew that he had put money in people's pockets and thought that this would give him allies. He was admitting in the village that he had hit Nothing and given them the reason: how many weeks pass and the girl would not open her knees, 'bout she mourning her father. And the old woman siding with her, saying is disrespect to be doing those things in a house that a person just pass from. What kind of foolishness that? How was he to make children? To this he added that the only reason they were behaving like this was because both of them, Miss Maud and the girl, had been sleeping with the man and the girl mightn't even have any womb, having thrown away children made by the man. The bad-minded ones added another meaning to "Nothing". Nothing could be made in Nothing's womb.

Mass Eustace's sister took him to court for a variety of things, slander and fraud included. With her Panama money and business sense she had known that she should hire a lawyer and she did. He heard that she had even tried to dissolve the marriage, and with that Everard ran away early one morning taking his truck with him. Cousin Nothing came into adulthood a fairly wealthy lady, still a teenager, for the lawyer had fixed it that not even marriage could get what Mass Eustace left her, away from her.

5. euphemia

Colón is not far from Hanover, so Hanover people used to leave home in their boats and go there to sell yam. Miss Phee, Euphemia, did not follow her brothers' gang and go to Clarendon; no cutlass and fork for her. Her tool was a sharp knife and a scale. She got a job with Jack Sprat and went in his boat to cut, weigh and sell yam. There she found out that the men were having difficulties with their laundry. Thus began a thriving back and forth of pants, shorts and even BVDs as Miss Phee added washing and ironing services to yam selling. After a while she thought to herself, why not set up a business in Colón instead of this backing and forthing. After all, there was no family left in Hanover, for all of them had gone off to some sugar estate out of the parish and some had even found their way to Central America.

She had heard of the famous doctress and said to herself, if she can go to these far places and set up hotel, what wrong why she can't do something as simple as wash clothes for men? She actually met the doctress, who told her that her idea was a good one and, better than that, she would give her work and allow her to gather a capital base with which to begin her business. Miss Phee didn't have to wait long before she was able to build herself a covered space, buy herself some big wash pans and scrubbing boards, put up drying lines, get in some iron boards and irons, and be ready for business. She already had the clients from when she was commuting from Hanover.

She carried over those from the doctress's business and before long was the place to find all the Jamaican men. Some would even come with the one suit on their backs, take it off and wait for Miss Phee to launder it. She had to build a special room for these naked men.

She couldn't manage this business by herself and, glad to help out the family, thought of inviting her little sister to come over. She would have loved to have her come and stay, but the child had followed the world of flesh and had chosen to make love-children by several men on the Clarendon estate to which she had gone with her brothers. All Miss Phee could do for her was take one of the girls, her sixteen-year-old daughter, and hope that unlike her mother she could take in more than man, could take something into her head. That sixteen-year-old niece was my grandmother.

The men over there couldn't handle Miss Phee: they called her a man-woman. She could manage a boat better than any of them. They had mostly grown up in the country among rivers; most of them couldn't swim strongly and were afraid of the large expanse of water that was with them daily. Euphemia could swim well. Where she had lived in Hanover was not far from the sea, and bathing and of course swimming in the sea was part of life. Colón was famous for mosquitoes and the diseases they brought. Miss Phee could take her cutlass and brush down the forest near to her, to discourage them. "Miss Phee, give me that job nuh," one of the men might say when they heard her chopping. "Jacob" or "Henry" or whoever, Miss Phee would address them: "Mi know you hand. It too saft fi this."

Much as they might have wished it, for Miss Phee was called "handsome", she had no inside job for any of them. "Ah white man you a wait pon," they would tease her. There were many of those and they too were now taking their clothes to Miss Phee. She asked all who were teasing, "Mi tell you sey mi want gold inside of me. Or even silver? Oonoo go wey. And mi no want none a oonoo saaf man eena me either. That something nuh mek yet that can get me fi mek a fool of myself over man."

My grandmother was not like her Aunt Euphemia. She was more like her mother, an ordinary woman, expecting a man to take care of her, to bring her gifts, to brush her yard, to limb her trees, following her smile and her beckoning finger. She wallowed in the compliments of the many men. To Miss Phee this young niece was a disappointment; she was a traitor and she was ready to send her back home but she couldn't find her. Her niece had run off with a silver man from America. There were a few there. My grandmother was taken in by the accent and the thought of somewhere else to go, for as with all the rest of the family, travel was in her blood; the world was her oyster. The silver man did not last long in Panama. When he was ready to go home and wanted her to come with him and bring their two children, somehow she heard that she couldn't walk on just any side of the street in his country and knew that she couldn't deal with that kind of restriction. Miss Phee took her back and sent her to live in the home of her twin brother, Mass Eustace, in Jamaica, where she and Cousin Nothing grew like sisters. It was good that they were so close for they were soon alone.

Miss Maud followed Mass Eustace soon after his passing, for it seemed she could not leave him alone. She had started their life together by harassing him about the fruit trees in the line. Then she had agreed with Pastor that he was responsible for the pregnancy of the half-witted girl and she had followed Nothing into his house. He had discovered that in spite of how much like a dragon she looked, she really was an innocent girl. She was really no more than ten years older than the girl Clarise, which made her a young girl of late twenties or early thirties to his fifty years. He could not deny that she was a hard and wise worker. It was through her that he had got his dasheen farm. Dasheen had walked over the line, and instead of quarrelling about it, she had offered to come over and show him the best places on his farm for encouraging them, for dasheen needed specially wet lands. She might be too big and tall for a photograph as a bride but she was young enough for marriage and they had gone off quietly to a marriage officer and got married. Pastor did not like that but he got his chance to feature when they turned thanks at his church. She pined after him. He was the only real company she had ever had, and seeing that the two girls were sensible and were company to each other, Miss Maud decided that life here didn't have much to offer her and she had better go to Heaven where she was likely to meet both Modibe and Eustace. She didn't go right away but kept getting lower and lower. It was as if she wanted to watch over the girls a little while before going. She was pure spirit by the time she went off to her men.

Everard had driven himself away before she went and it was now looking as if there was need for hands to keep the farm going, but my grandmother made it clear to all and sundry that she was not in that: the family had billed enough square grass to keep everyone happy until eternity. She would however make her contribution, she made the curious to understand. And what a contribution it was! Cousin Nothing had not continued with the banana business. Her father had been in the habit of planting a coconut tree for every one of her birthdays, so the farm had many of these, for Nothing kept on with this tradition. Women were not supposed to use the fork; coconuts would drop off the tree and sit wherever they fell and begin growing. By the time Nothing found them, they were already young trees. It didn't call for much digging with the fork to put them more firmly in the ground, so the farm was virtually a coconut estate. It was still so when I visited. That must have been why I wondered whether my parents' information and my mother's teasing was a story they made up, for it seemed to me that the name Conut could sensibly have had something to do with the coconut trees that filled her farm.

Nothing planted more coconuts and added to the sugar cane which her father had left her. Planting cane called for a little more effort. You definitely had to dig cane holes. Frail as she looked, Nothing, her back muscles being unusually well-developed, could manage this with the fork and got herself talked about again. Riding fork had made her barren, they said. Might be something in that, for Miss Phee produced nothing, Miss Maud produced nothing and here was Nothing also producing nothing, and all using the fork. Who knew anyhow if any seed had been planted but did not survive the journey to those wombs?

My grandmother had come back with a little money and she and Cousin Nothing agreed that she would buy all her coconuts and her cane. She knew the laundry business well, but who in the village could afford her? They all needed cooking oil and this is what she sold. My grandmother became a coconut oil maker. She also processed sugar cane into wet sugar and sugar head. Her sugar went into every baked delight she could think of. She was satisfying village needs as well as selling wholesale in the markets around. A fleet of donkeys left the home every Thursday evening to sell oil wholesale to higglers who retailed it in the markets. Baked goods and her sugar head went to every shop in the area on Fridays.

This basic outline I had got from Nothing and from my father. It would have been nice to put the sugar cane plant and the coconut in our mat but no one knew how to do this. Perhaps we could paint them on or embroider them on when the mat was finished, was Nothing's suggestion. Meanwhile we just made circles, each one an end and a beginning – circles of different sizes.

Everard, hearing that business was going on, came back to say that they needed him to market their products for them. My grandmother, who didn't really know him but was willing to trace his circumstances from what he looked like, having brought with her from Colón the notions of distinctions between people on the basis of colour – gold for white and silver for black – had asked him if he was mad; how could he come talking to black women about market which was in their blood when the only market he could possibly know was white people's factory, and she had no intention of having her energy sapped to feed them. Exit Everard.

My grandmother was not the kind who could do without a man nor could she see what was so great about being able to do without one on the inside of your life. Neville was old but not too old to make someone shiver. He had made it publicly known even as a twenty-year-old climbing the ladder to a headmaster's job, to whoever would listen, that he could have been Nothing's father if he had not been underdeveloped, so he intended to stick by her to the extent that she would let him. He was therefore a now-and-again visitor to the house. He did not live too far away and would visit on his horse, with his shoes so shine you could see your face in them. It was my grandmother Pearl who wanted to see her face those shoes and made clear her fascination with the schoolteacher.

People like Neville didn't get to college until they were well into their thirties. Neville had shown academic promise. He was just ten when Pastor had prepared him and sent him to take scholarship exam and he had got a half scholarship. Pastor intended for him to realize this promise. On his half scholarship at Thompson's, he had passed preliminary one and two. He was on his way to Mico Teachers College. He knew he could easily pass the entrance examination, but no one would be holding a place for him, so passing that exam had to go hand in hand with having the tuition and other fees. And where were those to come from? To help a person to a profession was a bouquet in someone's button hole. Other teachers were willing to help and Neville got little jobs as pupil teacher in their schools for several years before he approached the entrance exam. He did pass but not high enough, for there were no more than twenty places for hundreds of young men who wanted to do something more than swing a cutlass on an estate.

At his third try he met success and in three years he was a qualified teacher. He got a job close by to his home village and so was able to visit Nothing now and again and to hear news about her. One bit of news, not told to him but deduced, had him curious. He saw a tin can of coconut oil with a painting on its side saying "Eustace Reid Coconut Oil".

My grandmother was a stylish woman. Colón had exposed her to lots of styles, labelled things for instance. Milk came in a bottle with a label, so did hair oil and even soap. The labels made them pretty. She liked pretty things. Nothing could spend her energy planting food but Pearl would be planting flowers and tea bush and only those that smelt pretty. Her oil pans had to have style and so she painted the outside, painting her uncle's, the old man's, name upon them, out of respect for him who had died shortly after her return. Neville knew the name and came to find out what it was about. He offered his help and unlike Everard's, his was accepted. He had asked questions. How much do you pay for, and how much do you sell at, and what is your profit? No one knew. He gave them a lesson in profit and loss and offered to be their accountant. Clarise was his friend. This is the least he could do for her daughter, who could have been his if . . . . Miss Maud moving rapidly into the spiritual, remembered how close he had been to Nothing's mother and begged them to let him into their affairs. She was glad to see him and felt that with him around she could go on with her task of dying. Neville became the accountant to the businesses and visited often. In time they saw the point of his accounting and my grandmother saw that there was an attractive man around and made it clear that she was attracted.

He needed a woman. So many female assistant teachers to wade through and to separate; so many oversized teenage girl students, their mothers willing to arrange for you to seduce them so that they could blackmail you into marriage. Here was a woman who had travelled, with whom he could discuss world affairs, a woman not needing to share the little that government allowed a headmaster, for she had her own; a woman who could knead the knots out of your shoulder muscles and didn't mind doing that; a woman married already and therefore not needing to be broken in; a woman who could cook and bake, keep a flower garden, and who was delighted to have a man around. What should stop him? Wedding bells were soon ringing, and not long after that, they were making my father.

Neville arranged for the baking to be done in a specially constructed space and likewise the sugar making and oil making. He was worried about my grandmother's two children getting burnt while she was processing these products. This arrangement proved more fortuitous than he could have planned. Processing was going well, so was the farm and his teaching. He was invited to a bigger school with better pay and wanted my grandmother to come along. Not being Euphemia or Miss Maud or even Nothing, she was willing to drop everything and follow her man, but he thought it wasn't fair to leave Nothing like that. The farm depended on the factory. Must Nothing go now and find another market for her canes and her coconuts? With the business streamlined into sections and the accounting system set up, it was relatively easy for a manager to take over and to be supervised from afar. Neville found Theo and, as in the best romances of their time, Theo and Nothing hit it off well. They linked well on every scale and Nothing got another surname. It was Tull this time. She was still little and had Tull saying, as so many people had said before, that she really weighed nothing and couldn't have a more appropriate pet name. He was spellbound at Nothing's ability to work at farming as hard and as efficiently as he or any other man.

When my grandmother followed her husband to his new school, she and Nothing lost touch with each other. Not everyone could manage to write what was in their heart, so though there were post offices, not many letters flowed between them, and it really was Neville who was managing the business and going when he could to supervise, for the Lord had taken Tull in the thirteenth year of the marriage and nobody suitable had materialized. My grandmother was the housewife she wanted to be. My grandfather was all that a delicate flower or one who wanted to be a delicate flower could hope for. Neville even found a way of contacting Pearl's first husband and getting him to make American citizens of my father's half-brother and -sister. They did well under his tutelage and joined their father for college. Grandfather was now able to focus on his children. My aunt took to music and grandfather sent her to England to further her studies. They were happy that my father got into law school, for my aunt was a bit of a genius, and light-headed as such tended to be, and needed her brother to keep her sane. My father found a woman there but from home, to marry and to look after the children they made and also his talented sister.

Thus I was born in England. I was doing social studies in sixth form and needed to write a paper on the West Indian family. "What can be more West Indian than ours?" my father asked, and sent me off to visit my Jamaican relatives and write my paper. This is when I met my grandparents and when they took me down to meet Conut.

This is the basic outline of my A-level research. Some data I inferred from others and so on. But isn't that how science goes!

My presentation did not use the straight lines and arrows that one normally sees in family trees. I used the circles as in Conut's mat. My parents were a bit worried but they saw that it made sense and they felt that my teachers were flexible enough to give credit to innovation where it was useful. I got an A for my paper and learnt two new words – "iteration" and "recursion". I was not sure I knew what they meant then, but Miss had said that these were the principles we used in making the mat. "Your end is your beginning," she quoted from Conut and smiled. "In what odd places does wisdom reside," she added. "The literature speaks of the West Indian family as 'fractured'; you might be able to prove that it is a fractal" was the comment she made at the bottom of my paper. I knew this was a positive one and did not let the fact that it didn't make sense to me detain me. I was just happy to get my A, to have passed my exams and to be out of sixth form and on my way to university. It was a really unforeseen thing that caused me to be back in Jamaica.

I went home and refused to eat chicken. My mother was truly angry: her meal plans would go awry, for chicken was a staple of the household. It is funny how one thing loops back to another: one of the reasons for my mother's anger was that she feared I would get like my aunt, her husband's crazy sister. The only thing that Aunt Polly and I had in common as far as she or I or my father could make out was that we refused to eat chicken. In fact, Aunt Polly was a vegetarian. Only arty-crafty people who couldn't make a living in the world did not eat meat and were vegetarians. I was on my way, by my mother's argument, to being an arty-crafty person who would be unable to make a living.

I knew Aunt Polly but I didn't know about her. Aunt Polly did dress in her own style and was a singer of classical music, not the kind of thing sensible black people in England did. Seems she wasn't too successful in this career, a career *change* actually, for her piano playing was a non-starter as far as making a living was concerned. My genius aunt had come to England to study piano. She had been a child prodigy in Jamaica. This didn't translate in England, where there were several child prodigies. It seemed too that as Aunt Polly grew out of childhood, the prodigy part of her faded and she became a woman struggling for attention as an artist. And there were enough of these too in England. Since she was black, she was supposed to sing, not play the piano: Aunt Polly turned to singing the jazz that black women were supposed to sing. She would go off now and again on a tour, but what she brought back couldn't buy her a flat, or even pay the rent, so my father often had to help her out. She had been on his wing, it seemed to my mother, forever and she wished she would grow up and get a job as a clerk in some store, dress properly, straighten her hair and stop this vegetarianism and music. And of course stop frightening my mother that she would be my model.

It was Aunt Polly who noticed that I wasn't heaving and sighing. It was the time for asthma in London and I didn't have an attack, though my father did have his bouts. Aunt Polly put this down to my chicken-less diet. My mother is a nurse and of course was glad that one of her charges no longer had to depend on medication to breathe, but she still would not credit the source. When she heard Nothing's story about my grandmother, she flew so high, I thought she would end on the carpet dead like that life-saving fowl. She wished she could prevent me from accepting my aunt's invitation to lunch but how stupid it would seem if my aunt could not invite me to celebrate my success in my GCEs.

At this lovely Indian restaurant we had our curried vegetables and girl talk.

"What's happened to that young man whose eyes used to follow you around?" she asked as soon as we were settled.

"That Cousin Nothing experience has so taken me over that I cannot now return his gaze."

"Don't let that happen. I applaud the GCEs and all that but don't join the band of manless women that is in your family line."

"Aunt Polly you are manless and I don't see anything wrong with you."

"Your mother does not agree and she might be right."

"And by the way, why is my mother so negative about my father's family?" I ask.

"Your mother is negative about word of *everybody's* family. Did she encourage you to do her family tree? Have you ever met anyone from her side? I know she is said to have a sister but thereon hangs a tale. Did she tell you to check any of her relatives when you went to Jamaica?" The answer was no. She continued: "And didn't you find that funny?"

I had to admit that I just didn't think of it. My father's family has been so much the talk in the house that I couldn't find space to ask about anybody else.

"I am annoyed that I am the one to tell you this but your mother is a foundling."

I had to repeat the word. "Foundling?" Such a word I only met in books. A baby is wrapped in a blanket, put in a straw basket and left at the door of a church, to be discovered and adopted by some childless wife in the congregation, and it is later found out that this was her baby by another man, a baby her sterile husband was unable to give her, born just before he came back from the war or wherever. What a romantic story my mother was involved in! But I was to learn that it was nothing of that kind. She had just been left on a bridge and it was the mercy of God that saved her. Whoever left her there must have expected a bus, truck or other vehicle to crush her to death, for she was left in the middle of the road. There had been no basket, straw or otherwise. A domestic servant on her way to work had found her and taken her to the police station. From thence she was taken to a government place of safety, where they named her Bridget, for there was no name lovingly pinned to her chemise as with foundlings in books and "Bridget" did carry her history as surely as "Windsor" carried the queen's. An attendant, liking her, and needing a playmate for her own daughter, short-circuited the legal procedures and took her home. She had to adopt her officially when she got the ward maid job in England and decided to migrate.

"It is not that she hates your father's family," my aunt explained. "It is just that she hates her own story. Your father and I know that, and since she has been good to us, allow her to trash our family without pointing to hers. You will notice that he does not rebuke her." My aunt ended as she did most communications, "She'll be all right; you'll be all right and we all will be all right."

My mother is a nurse. Found on a bridge she may have been, but she is nobody's fool. Despite her vexatious words, she had told one of the specialists in her hospital about my not eating chicken and my new state of health. I was now hearing that I must have had an allergic reaction to chicken, and she was wondering if my father and I shared that allergic gene and would he try going off chicken. He did and it worked. That was the end of the bad-talking of Cousin Nothing and my father's crazy family. I could now interrogate them with some blessing from her. Better than that: the university in Jamaica was a college of London University and it had a good reputation for family studies. I asked the administration if I could go to study there and they had no difficulty with the concept. I asked my parents and they were okay with the idea, for I would still be getting a London degree. My father teased, "Be careful that you don't get lost in one of those recursions in the Nth iteration and cannot find your way back to the right side."

Conut was still alive but the mat was not finished. There was still string hanging and it would do so to infinity unless someone decided to stop the journey. Keith had died. I don't know what kind of funeral service he had, but if there was to be a eulogy inside or outside of church, it could not be better than what Miss Cookie had to say about the matter.

"God send that boy here for a purpose – to teach people not to go into their neighbour field and dig out their things. Miss Nothing did not know half the story; she didn't know that no tiefing happen again from that child born and people know his state. The Master once asked his disciples, when they told him of a certain tragedy, if they thought what happened to those people happened because God thought they were worse sinners than anybody else. He told them that God was merely using those people and their tragedy as a lesson to others, and that the others better hear that message, for it could be worse with them. Perhaps if Miss Nothing didn't keep the boy around, tiefing might have kept on happening, but from she take him in, everybody know that the message is alive and that they should take heed. God bless her for taking care of His message." What I knew was that now that she had done this work, Nothing could safely die. She was waiting for me to come back, they said; she wanted me to put on her stockings to complete her dress for her coffin. This frightened me a bit: her feet and my hands, the end being the beginning. Was I really going to be lost in a recursion, as my father had joked? I did dress her for her funeral and here I am. There was nothing to be afraid of.

I added Turnbury in my mind to the mat. As Everard's father had been passionate about rum, so had he been passionate about the Lord; he had joined the Reverend Henderson's Tabernacle at Brown's Town and believing that he had done Nothing and her father a wrong, he had willed his Turnbury to his wife June Reid. This Turnbury, my grandparents told me when I arrived in Jamaica, this time to do the master's, Nothing had willed to me along with all the sisal strands that we had created from the ping wing macca on my first visit. I was an owner of real estate. I was landed, perhaps even gentry. And at twenty-one! I didn't take up ownership or even come to see the place, just luxuriated in the thought that I owned real estate. I left my grandfather to do the transfer of the title and other formal and legal issues while I went on to a terminal degree. I know he appreciated this swap. He was doing mundane things like paying the taxes while I got another degree, even if that did not make me *the first black to* . . . . Here I am, Dr Something, with no conference to go to and electing to be in the Turnbury house, sitting on my daybed, depressed and hoping that remembering will raise my spirits. I remember Aunt Polly and I remember the fellow's gaze. I have to admit to myself that I am sorry that I stopped returning his gaze; it is lonely here. It is the long summer holiday and I have no conferences to go to, no friends from home visiting. I think I will just finish Cousin Nothing's mat. This little tiled veranda could do with it for it does get a bit chilly in December. There is sisal left over from those days. This is really strong material. Why do we buy cord when we can make this? I shall put in the details that Cousin Nothing did not know about. In my head, I will stick them around the circumference of the mat and give it and me closure.

part 2.

6. maud and modibe
morant bay, 1865

If you live at Stony Gut, it is nothing for you to walk into Morant Bay. And Bay had good market for you to buy and sell, and if you didn't want to buy or sell, you could go to the courthouse and get plenty jokes. Those people arrest us and carry us to court for nearly everything. Sammy today, you tomorrow, for doing nothing but breathing, so you had to go to courthouse not just for joke but to know how to conduct yourself, for any day it would be your time to come before the magistrate.

Bay was a place where you meet everybody. I was particular about one of the Africans. He was not really born in Africa but his mother and father were. They had plenty manners and they worked hard: good people. It helped that they had come on contract and could get a piece of land when they finished their five years. Many bought additional lands so that those Africans became the top of the top, but even so they had problems with already-rich people for they wanted to cheat them out of the land that the contract that bring them to Jamaica say they must get. One of the sons was looking at me and I wanted him to keep on seeing me and locking eyes with me for I was saving myself for a decent marriage with him.

That Saturday they were charging a boy no older than my sixteen years and people came out to protect him for God knows they woulda kill him and us like rat if we didn't keep our eyes open. They charge the boy four shillings and told him that he had to pay three times that extra – twelve shillings and sixpence for something they call "processing" fee. A man call out from the back of the courthouse, "Pay the four shilling only. The twelve shillings and sixpence is pure tiefry. Don't pay that." The officers in the courthouse tell him to shut up but that only make him shout out his message more loudly. Then they step forward as if they are going to hold him and he run, still bawling out, "Only pay the four shillings. The rest is tiefry." Everybody start laugh and then when the officers start run after the man, the whole of us get up and start run after the officers. It was a sight! This little-'fraid-running-after-big-'fraid procession had was to stop for there was another case to try. The officers wipe their faces and pull down their shirts and walk back to the courthouse, we behind them. The magistrate hit his table for silence and we all go quiet.

Monday come and we go back again to the courthouse. This time it full up of us. I didn't even know that this was the big case that had brought so many to the courthouse. This one had to do with Daddy B's cousin and you don't play with that family for Daddy know his words, he know his Bible and he know the law. Same thing happen like the Saturday case. This time is Daddy B bawl out tell Brother Miller, his cousin, not to pay. Must appeal the case. Fool-fool officer do the same thing them did before. Dem can't see that is ten of them and about three hundred of us? Dem start show off, go to Daddy wielding them baton and telling him to shut up. Who? Daddy B, who could talk for one night straight without even drinking water! Dem put them hand on him and three hundred people surround them. Them give up baton and turn to pen and paper. Start write down name of who dem sey obstructing them in the line of dem duty.

By the time we reach back home, fool-fool officer in dem uniform that-is-not-fi-dem-money-buy reach up to Stony Gut. Black one dem send, as if that mean anything to wi, for wrong is wrong. If dem couldn't arrest wi in the courthouse, how dem going to arrest wi in wi owna place when more people is here than was in the courthouse? Daddy B was in his chapel praying. He come out to them and say, "What? Oonoo want to make me Jesus now? Coming into my garden to arrest me while I am praying." And him cuss dem off worse: "Look your colour and you want to handle your

people so, for the sake of white people and dem ignorant law." He preach
it to them. He ask them if they ever hear about Jesus Christ, the only thing
good in white, though nobody too sure since nobody see him. He told them
that Jesus Christ was the champion of the poor and downtrodden and who
was more downtrodden than us black people in Stony Gut.

He remind them of how many people's little piece of land get stolen by
the big white people and they don't see to protect their own people from
them. He preach it, tell them that is just because black people now turning
to their God, and rather starve upon their knees before their God than go
fork up them dutty dry ground, that you see them get so vicious pon us. He
tell them he cannot serve God and Mammon and neither should they. He
invite them to pray, kneel and pray.

I will admit that they got very much help in getting to their knees but
while they were there, they stayed there, while Daddy B prayed over them
and some other deacon add their voices too and some of us kneel and pray
with them too. We were not just faking it. Daddy told us they were our
brothers and we should help them with our prayers. We were accustomed
to doing that for with the revival, not a man, woman or child go to them
bed with a vexation towards them brother or sister. The least little curse-
out we have, you see man and man gone down on their knees together and
start to ask each other pardon and ask God for strength to help them do
right. When the officers dem feel they get enough salvation, they get up
and go about their business. Daddy was right. He say to all, while they were
leaving, "A just man is not made overnight. We will have to go down to Bay
and tell them down there what happened here, for the forces of evil that
these people deal with every day and night will not allow justice to flow like
the river that it should."

Daddy B say we must go down in an orderly way. So the men form up
in four lines and the women line up in those same lines but behind them.
We know that the big heads, the vestry them call themselves, was going to
meet, so we was going to see them and put our side of the story to them.
We was walking down orderly but the wicked mad to see how we orderly,
an dem line up man with gun to face wi. Our men did have cutlass. Daddy
never tell anybody to carry cutlass but you ever see earth man without him
'lass? Suppose him going uphill and he have to cut a walking stick? Suppose
somebody mule losing him shoe, he take that cutlass edge and screw it on

back. Sometimes he use the broad side of the 'lass to brush away a bad dog, and those who can write might put a piece of paper on the 'lass and write like on a desk or table. I never see even one soul sharpen a 'lass that day. And man was holding his 'lass in the crook of his arm like how people carry young baby. Nobody was threatening them down there in Bay. We was just walking decent and them surprise. I don't tell you that anything we do wrong in those people's eyes. So dem start to fire because we look too decent and orderly. We must be up to something bad if we in line instead of walking raggedy-raggedy and a skin and a grin like a set of donkeys eating cane, skinning and grinning so that they can say, "Look the asses. Grinning. Don't even know when people taking advantage of them."

The man dem nearly fi turn back but the woman dem sey, "Not a blast of this. Oonoo nah lef we one fi deal with them an dem have to deal with." And dem get real vile when dem see that the man dem what drop, really dead. Dem take off dem skirt leave only dem petticoat and them full up dem skirt with stone and start to pelt the gunman dem. Di woman dem pelt stone and dem say, "See free stone yah. When oonoo hire wi fi find stone and break it, oonoo no pay wi. See free stone ya." Free stone win out. It hurt dem worse when the said people dem who owe dem and can well pay them, come out and call them out of them name without them title, and ah sey like, "Amy, I am surprised at you. You are always a peaceful person. Let peace reign." Dem answer back, "You want peace now but is justice we want." And some of them correct them and say like, "And this is Mrs Allen to you; Amy for my friends. You ever see me calling your wife anything but Mrs Cooke? I know she name Daisy but I dare not call her that. Give me my title please."

Then my whole world turn upside down for who was coming down the road happy as pappy, with a set of his people from a side road, but Modibe. Dem Africans have a way of running like dem going fall on them face. Same way dem coming down and it pretty so 'til and is my Modibe leading them. He have his cutlass in the air but that is how dem do when dem happy. He shouting something that sound like *Manalva* but I know is "Nana Reba" he say, for he explain it to me. It mean "the Queen is coming". No more queen was coming than me. His eye lock on me and I feel like today is the day when our two families going to do the joining. I start to broke-waist dance towards him saying that I ready, he can make appeal to my father, den "bow". Him drop before I could reach him. I bawl you see and I hate them, hate them, man. Hate them can't done. Mi see a woman with a piece of wood with fire pon it. One of them that call themselves "volunteer" order her to bring it to him to light his pipe. Mi start drag bramble, put by the little house where them coward which call themselves the bigger heads run gone hide. I take the lady's fire-stick and I catch the bramble and other people join in, some ah blow fire and some ah put coconut coir pon it to make the fire come up fast. Me do that. Me start fire. My father come and find me and lead me away, so I don't know if dem burn up fi true eena the little school room and the courthouse, or if is true that we kill how much of them but dem deserve it. Set a wicked them!

A funeral is not a thing to hurry up. The leave-taking, for instance, is slow. Though Modibe and me never really get to pledge, his people did know that that was in his heart, so they make me lead the leave-taking. Mi ah dance mi funeral dance going slow from this house to the next with Modibe box behind me and the crowd after that, wheeling at the crossroads and so on, like mi know mi should do, when who shoulda hold me but the same officer dem that did come for Daddy B. I did really think those maroon people did know more respect. There they was with the officer dem molesting the funeral procession! Hear one of them nuh, "Who you saving it for dead an gone." And there and then without respect for himself nor me nor the people around, nor for the spirit going home, the man throw mi down on the ground, lift up me dress and have his way with me and 'bout six more of them, with dem bulge can't stay in dem pants, partake of me, me a virgin. I tell you my front so sore, I couldn't pee for days. My mother take me and put me to bed. Fever hot like what upon me. She draw fever grass and sopping mi body and have me drinking garlic tea.

Mi father and Modibe's father come into the room and though them see mi wrap up under the thick sheet my mother did just make from calico and crocus bag dem sey from wherever mi fi get the strength from, me better get ready fi walk miles to my safety and them sey moreover, Modibe little sister coming with me. She only seven but dem man de no mind age. Dem will come back for her. Dem sey people did see mi wid the fire and mi name write down and dem sure fi come fi me and dem people no shame fi heng woman. Mi mother start pack fi me. Give me two heads of garlic and tell me must keep on eating it. It will burn but not to mind that for it will cure the sores that the man dem leave on me and clean me out too. She beg them to wait little bit for Ma Lou to come for she send for her already. Ma Lou is a healer lady, not just the body. She cure the spirit too. Ma Lou come but she couldn't do the whole ceremony for she too have to run, and she tell the man dem that them have to run. All the other man dem gone up into the hills to hide and them mustn't take brave and stay there. Mi beg them if me coulda come with them but they say no, the whole of the maroon dem turn 'gainst us and them know sey is not long before dem going catch dem and do wha them want with them. "No," mi father definitely sey for dem abuse him already by doing that to his daughter before his face; dem coulda heng me before him face and him can't deal with that.

Now we never had much need to leave Stony Gut. We go Bay often but that is just like going to Stony Gut. I never even go to Monklands much less Kingston but Cherry Gardens in Kingston is where my father and Modibe's father think I should try to go. Say I must avoid the mountain for soldier coming down from Newcastle by those mountains and that is where the maroon dem live. Must keep to the coast. Just make sure that I see the sea all the time and I will reach Kingston and after Kingston must try to get to St Ann. In Kingston I must ask for the Tabernacle. They will keep me there and when I feel I am able to move on to St Ann, ask the same thing when I reach there. So mi get up mi courage eena mi hand and dem get food for me to carry. Pan of drinking water, some bake left over from plenty people breakfast and some jackass corn mi mother did make fi sell for she is a baker. Journey could take long, they say, so dem give me uncooked food that can last: yam and dasheen that mi can roast. Worse come to the worse they say, mi could even sell them. So me sixteen and don't know much, set out with the basket of ground provisions on my head and the little seven-year-old girl carrying the shut pan of water and a towel with the baked food under her arm. We have on two suits of clothes. That suit me for you know how when you have fever, you feel cold. So it suit me to have on the nuff clothes but the little girl must be did hot with all that clothes on her. Nevertheless, she look brave. Mi front a hurt me but mi step high like mi know where mi going and mi glad to go, for mi know them watching mi and perhaps a cry.

Mi tek bush, the little girl behind me. Mi look round and see her a pick something. Ah, just the bird suck vine and she a pick off the bird suck and put it in her mouth. Mi slap it out of her hand and shake her hard by the shoulders. Now bird suck is not something anybody can sell. Is not like coffee or even mango; is just something pickney and bird like, but them people will lock you up if you pick anything off of anybody property. De child vex but me can't take that on for as mi tell her mi is now her mother and she have to listen to what me say and obey. Then mi realize that me now have to behave certain way so that she can respect what me say and obey me, me who don't even know what leaf good for what sickness. But Daddy B did tell we that we have to have faith in ourselves; and Ma Lou did tell me that plenty good spirit out there that will show me things; said that Modibe would be with me, so mi press on. Mi tell the child nuh fi trouble nothing but mi had was to trouble, for mi see two bunka drop off a one tree, just right fi she sleep in and mi sleep in and mi take them up. The little girl start to ask me how come me can do it, mi tell her sey me ah big somebody and can go to jail and as a matter of fact, mi will carry the two bunka so if anybody see we with them is me them going arrest. The little girl sey den is how she going manage if dem arrest me, so better the two of us get arrest, so she want to carry one of the bunka dem. Nice little girl.

Now bunka is a thing that drop off of a tree that look like a coconut tree, though they call it cabbage tree. I couldn't see why, for it don't look anything like cabbage. These bunka dem come in all sizes. Those of us who have no barbecue use them to put coffee and chocolate to dry and sometimes people use them as baby bed. These two that drop off and I pick up, is like them drop off for us, for is a big one and a small one, and that show me that good spirits was really with us. Dem never easy to carry for them hard to roll up but we couldn't advertise that we have them so we have to take energy and roll them and put them on wi head under the basket that mi carrying and under the shut pan that she carrying. The bush we walk through is really only me and she. It quiet bad. Is daybreak and people supposed to be walking going to them field and so on but it quiet and nobody not walking about. Mi no think too much about that, mi jus press on. Me come to cross-roads and mi no ask no question, mi just go like mi mind tell me and walk like mi know where mi going. But mi smell the sea and mi know that mi taking the right path.

The beach like it have some things like cave can keep off the rain. We go into one of these with wi bunka and this is where and when we eat our first meal and drink little water. The little girl's head start roll on her shoulder, so mi put her out flat to sleep and me watch, for me couldn't sleep. Before dawn mi see one something – look like ship, though mi never see ship yet. White man come off it in white uniform. Mi tell the little girl not to make no noise and wi stay in the beach cave. We stay there the whole day. Is night before we start out again, walking through bush but keeping our eyes and nose seeking out the sea.

One time mi find a pepper tree. Mi don't know who tell me but mi pick the leaf dem and start rub them in mi hand and find that it feel like cloth. Mi put it on the sores on my front and it make walking a little easier for, with me legs brushing against each other, the sores that the man dem leave me with feel like them getting raw. Mi find leaf of life what everybody know is the cure for head and chest cold and mi mek her put it in her dress and eat it as we go, for with we out in the night she coulda get bad cold and what me woulda do? Something start to happen to me: mi feel like liquid running down mi legs. When mi look is like corruption. The pepper leaf bring the sores to a head and cause the poisons to start to leak out of my body. There and then mi start walk easier. So mi learn one thing: pepper leaf can heal. All this time mi no stop eat the garlic and the little girl no stop eat the leaf of life. Night come and we find another sea cave and sleep. Me sleep this time too. We wake up next morning and find that we beside two separate ponds, each big like sea and them smell like salt but them brown; them don't blue like sea. We now have to come off the beach and walk on the path. Plenty other females walking and them start up conversation with us and me tell them that mi is a higgler and the girl is my sister and we going to Kingston to market. Dem notice certain things and ask mi if is my first time and mi tell them yes, and they say just follow what we do.

So much river to cross! Mi glad mi with them for it look like them travel this road often and know just where the water light enough for people to walk over. We reach a place dem tell us name, Rockfort. It pretty so 'til! The blue-blue sea close by the road and when you look straight in front of you, you see nothing but sea must be all even gone to Africa. When you look to your left side you see a little strip of road beside a sea that have small islands in it like stepping stones which God put there so that He could walk a short pass from the salt pond to the strip of land, and then to the right hand side you see like a whole continent. There the women tell me is where Kingston is. It would be nice if we could just swim to Kingston but mi can't swim and mi sure the little girl can't swim either. When mi look behind me is one mountain look like it touch the sky and it look like it would be a good place to hide but me remember that dem sey is into mountain that maroon live, so even if somebody did give me wings and say *fly to safety in those mountains*, me wouldn't go. The woman dem say that is where they stopping so me and the little girl have to press on by wi-self. Nothing else you can do besides put one foot before the other and give thanks that we reach so far.

We still have little water into the pan and I going tell you how we come to lose it and how mi come fi frighten fi de gal. We reach one place wid plenty potato slip. Dem call it Barbican, dem tell wi. We see something we never see yet: somebody black like wi but dem hair straight like the Baron and dem other rich people. That man don't wear clothes like them though: him body wrap up into cloth. Tell the truth me was wondering how somebody pee in clothes like that when the man start peel off the clothes. Mi turn away mi head for me no want see any more man privates. When mi tink the man finish and me turn round me head, nuh see the little gal hand eena de man hand like him a carry the child's hand to him privates and she a look down pon it like a some Christmas plaything. Me did tired an a sit down on the grass. Mi no know where mi get the energy from but mi tek up the pan of water that the child leave on the ground and run go over to them and land the bottom edge of the pan into the man head; him drop and all of the little water we have left splash out of the pan on the man. Mi can't understand what the man say but it sound like him sorry so mi just grab up the gal. Mi shake her and give her one big thump and ask her if she is a alabaster dolly baby what backra pickney play with or if she have sense. Mi wonder to myself, Ah, what dis dem give mi fi tek care of! How mi ago manage this? After mi myself don't even know nothing 'bout man except that dem bring you pain.

Now all wi have left is the yam and dasheen. This same man see mi a try fi light fire, come fi help mi and mi never run him. We give him piece of the yam and him give wi piece of him fresh fish, then mi take the gal hand and mi start run. Him never try to follow us. Then wi see one black lady look something like Ma Lou and she ask mi what mek wi a run so out of breath, and mi tell her about the man and ask her about Tabernacle. She say that is just a coolie man and him not going trouble us and she tek wi to Tabernacle and there she ask us if we bring anything. Mi show her the ground provisions and she say she know where we come from for is only there have dasheen. Then them want to know what happen down at Bay. Mi tell them what me know but them know more than we. Is from them mi hear how court house burn down and white men get killed and how them hanging our people like dem is dog. Dem sey the least them can do is look after we.

Mi father did tell me that mi can leave Kingston and go to St Ann when mi ready. Mi never ready for a long time. Mi stay with the Tabernacle people for they were just like back at Stony Gut. What them deal mostly in is potato. Mi jook slip into ground; mi dig fi potato and tek to market. Di gal foot to foot with me so she learn how to manage provision ground. Is the going to the market with her that was troubling. The one thing me know must not happen to that girl, if mi nuh want Modibe fi come back come kill me fi him little sister, is make what happen to me wid the maroon man dem happen to that girl, but it was hard. Seem the little gal was looking for that trouble. She see man ah piss, she gaan look. One woman one day say to me, "If we was in the old country" – and mi know where she was talking – "certain parts of that girl privates cut off and your problem stop. But we can't do that here." So what is the point of telling me that, since it can't be done here? Me still don't have no solution to the problem, but at least mi know now sey is not me one see that the child mad about man. Me say to myself, "Too much man in Kingston. Perhaps dem don't have so much at St Ann and is so mi start to think of how to get to St Ann. No problem really, for the Tabernacle people find them market woman friends and them put us with them and we set out.

7. clarise

I have a nice name, though if you were to listen to her you would believe my name was "Gal". While my mother was carrying me, she was working in Backra Fitzherbert's house and they had a houseguest who liked her and asked that the baby, if it was a girl, take her name. The name was Clarise and it was pronounced so that the end sounded like you were saying *ease*, *"ease my body"*. I didn't really know her well, this woman who sey she is in charge of me, and I don't know if she knew me. I knew about her, though, for Modibe used to talk about her and tell me that I should love her for she was going to be my sister. How can someone be "going to be" your sister. You sister is born your sister. Modibe is a big person and I suppose he knows what he was saying, so this female who say she was in charge of me must be my sister. She was all right when we set out but I didn't like it when she haul me up and shake me for eating the bird suck that not even the bird don't want any more. Then with the strange man, she hit me, though she later take fish from him, and at the market when I look at the men, some of them reminding me of Modibe and of my father, she hit me and I don't like it at all for I don't even understand why she want to do this. She keep on saying that why she hit me is that she didn't want what happen to her to happen to me. But she would never tell me what happen to her. But sometimes when we were in the cave on the beach, she would put her hand around my shoulder. That feel good and I feel like I have a mother. Also I know that she wasn't sleeping most of the time we were in the sea cave, but instead watching over me. Odd person. Is after the strange man that she start to call me "Gal". That time she curse me and tell me that me useless like alabaster baby and she don't know what she going to do with me for is like me don't have any sense.

I get good treatment while I was in Kingston at the Tabernacle and I didn't want to leave for St Ann with her, but everybody say must go. Who would I stay with? Couldn't stay alone, though since I am there I pass through five New Year's Days, so I must be a big girl now. I couldn't go back to Stony Gut to my family even if I could manage the trip by myself; for one thing, all of them dead, so I hear, so we set out again like the children of Israel in the wilderness. I know about that for Daddy B used to keep school and we read it in the Bible and then again here at Tabernacle there was school and we read the Bible.

We leave Kingston at the beginning of the year. I know that, for that is the time when the John Cunnu used to come out. I frighten as usual, for she tell me that if I don't stop looking at man, the John Cunnu going to take me with them. But I couldn't stop looking for my father and my brother among the men. From what I hear the big people say, all the black people at Stony Gut dead. I know that those killer people them take away the body of my father and my brother but I know about spirit and I know that spirit can enter into other bodies. I know my father and brother spirit is strong and will go into other bodies, so that is why I was looking at men, to see if the spirit of my father and my brother gone into any of them. But she don't know about that; she only know that man bad and will do you harm, so she don't want me to look at any of them and I think she set up John Cunnu to frighten me. One year the devil really did come up to me with his fork and nearly jab me with his big three-pronged fork.

Like when we were leaving Stony Gut, they full us up with food. We still have the two bunka skin. We always sleep on it and now it soft and easy to fold like it is cloth. This time we have two big bankra, the kind that look like hamper, the way the two sides hang down over our ears and our head just sit there in the middle. We have all kind of baked foods and plenty water, this time in enamel shut pans for they mostly use enamel in town, not tin pans. Apart from this, she carry in her bankra, dasheen that she pull out of the ground. She couldn't leave dasheen alone. She did keep back one when we just reach Town and she chop it up and plant it and it really bear. When she take it to the market, people rush for it and they start to call her the "dasheen woman". She must be like that name, and feel she have to plant it anywhere she go.

She tell me we moving on to Spanish Town. Now I know Spanish is a language and a kind of people, so I kind of worried for I am shy and feel I am not going to be able to deal with these people, but it wasn't so. I didn't see any different kind of people nor hear any sentence that I couldn't understand. They don't talk of "Tabernacle", though; they talk about "chapel". We find our way to the chapel and this time she talk plain: she tell the man in charge our true story and say that her father and my father say that we are to go to St Ann where they will look after us. They agree to look after us until we ready to go and they find us place to sleep and give us work to do. Meanwhile she tell me that our life is going to change, for when we reach St Ann we are going to stop moving; we are going to settle down; we are going to keep house and we have to start buying things for house. Look like she have money leave over from Cherry Gardens, which is where we was in Kingston, for she go out and buy basin pan. Nice, nice with flowers. She say is enamel. She buy goblet to match and chamber pot. How we going to carry these things, I wonder, but I don't say anything for I don't want to be called fool-fool alabaster baby. She want to buy pig but she couldn't find any, so she buy fowls: two – a rooster and a hen.

One day they call us and say a cart going to Linstead early the next day and that is not far from St Ann and we could get a ride there. Her enamelware she stack one into the other and say she will carry that, for if I carry it, I might let it fall and it would chip up and she don't want to quarrel with me. I am wondering how she is going to carry the fowls. This lady, who call herself my sister and sometimes my mother, tie up the feet of the fowls and then tie them to each other. She don't put them down. She throw them around her neck like somebody else would wear a necklace. Her bosom big and so the two fowls just lie down upon it. When we get into the man's cart, she still have the fowls around her neck. She have corn in her hand and they pecking the corn out of hand middle. I don't know how she stand that.

When place pretty is like my foot cannot move and I have to stand still and feel the place. They have a bridge that cross a river there, and when

you on that bridge, you wouldn't mind if it break down with you and you
become a part of the water and the flowers in the water and the shadows of
trees that you see in the water. I am leaning out of the cart to better feel this
thing when she rush me up again, about how she can't swim so I better sit
down carefully for she is not jumping into any river to save me. But guess
what I hear her say is, *What a pretty place. I could really just stay here all of my
life.* And I remember the time when we were going into Kingston and she
could hardly lift up her foot to walk on for she wanted to watch the blue-
blue sea and the stepping-stone islands. So I know that is not me alone love
pretty place and that loving pretty place don't make you an alabaster baby,
for she love them too. So she really not as hard and strange as she want me
to believe.

   We never even know which part of St Ann we going to but they say
that according to what we tell them, where we looking for is Sturge Town.
So we get ride and we come off at a place the man driving the cart say is
Linstead. I hear him say to her that he don't have a wife and that we could
come and stay with him. She just going on as if she don't hear him and start
taking our things off the cart. Me woulda did go with him but him didn't
ask me. Same way many men in Cherry Gardens there in Kingston put this
question to her and she either vex up and walk off or just laugh. Seems like
she don't want help from any man. So now instead of staying in Linstead
with the man, we walking around with bankra on our head and the two
fowls around her neck, looking for the way to St Ann. They show us a road
and not far up there we see people carrying stone. She ask what it is for and
she hear that is a church – they call it "church" – setting up, and straightway
she know that that is where we should be. Place they say is named Jericho
and when she tell them what she looking for in St Ann, they say is Sturge
Town we looking for. We stay with the Jericho people and carry stone with
them and luck take us again, for somebody was going to Sturge Town. We
riding high this time for is carriage that was going to Sturge Town. She still
with fowl around her neck in the people's carriage. Lucky none of them
doodoo on her in the people dem carriage. They leave us there with the
parson. Him give us work again and she give him some of her dasheen
and plant it for him. I hear him tell her say him not going to give her any
money in her hand for our labour, but he will put up the money that he
would pay her into an account and she can buy a little bit of land with it

when land come up for sale. Is that time she find that she need to give us a last name. The people at Cherry Gardens in Kingston did tell us that like how the government have down her name because she did help set the fire at Morant Bay, they would still be looking for her. They would know her by her father's name so she must change her last name. She give us a name that somebody in the Tabernacle have. So now we name Clarise Walker and Maud Walker.

I notice that people don't usually ask you question about yourself; to do so is bad manners. They make a statement about you and ask you if is true. They would say to her for instance, "Is your little girl this. Right?" and she would nod a yes. If they say, "Is your little sister this?" is the same answer they get. If they make such a statement to me, I know I must not answer but leave them to her. This is how it go even when we reach Sturge Town, which is where we were to go from the time we left Stony Gut. All now I don't know for sure what she is to me – sister or mother. I don't suppose it really matter.

Land come up, for somebody dead and didn't get to pay off for it and he have no living soul to do it for him, so it share up amongst who can pay off his debt and we get one little piece with the money Pastor was holding for her and they help us to build a one-roomed house. They make "join a corner" bed for us and we put our bunka on that for our sleeping, and she and me start to plant mostly dasheen. The rooster and the hen make noise but that did not matter for everyone else have fowl. Many fowls and they keep up noise too. The hen start to lay. So now we have eggs and is my job to search for the eggs, for the hen would drop them anywhere. The fowl make so much noise when she lay that it was not a hard job. It became even easier when she split a piece of bamboo, lean it up against the house and put some banana trash in it. The fowl would jump up and sit there and lay her eggs. How did the fowl know that she was to lay there? We didn't eat all the eggs; she keep back some for the fowl to set on so she could make chickens. When the little chickens come, it is my job to see that mongoose don't eat them off. She get a chance to bawl after me again, for she worried that I will step on the chickens and kill them. That was easy to do for the little things would run all around me and sometimes I don't know where they are, and if I don't turn around carefully, I could find one of them under my foot. I didn't step on any of them, though. Dem fowls was my friends even after I find Neville. I call them with a special sound and they would come to me. They knew me.

I like this settling down, so much so that I wasn't remembering Modibe and my father so much. I go to church and I like that. I get plenty nice clothes from the church box and I have my friend, Neville. He was too small for my father or Modibe's spirit to get into him but I watch him pee anyhow and we talk about his thing and mine and we link sometimes. Mass Eustace live near to us and I don't know why him and she must quarrel so! I think she is quarrelling with him just because he is a man. I don't know why he is quarrelling with her. He always complaining that she pick what she shouldn't pick and she claiming that it is in the line and she have a perfect right to it. And I remember what I do not want to remember: how I pick the bird suck and how she drag me away say they will arrest me for tiefing people things. But even if it was just to come and quarrel, I was glad to see Mass Eustace, for he look like maybe my father's spirit could be in him and I like to have a man's spirit around me, better still if it could be my father's spirit. Then he behave like a little boy and I have a baby and Parson say is because he behave like a little boy.

Is not all the time I did like the baby but sometimes she was nice to play with. Then I got sick and they say I would die and I didn't mind, for I would be with Modibe and my father, but I was wondering whose body would my spirit get into and I was thinking that it would go into the little girl, for why else did I have her? She was my friend and I liked to walk around with her with my breast into her mouth. When she get teeth now, we stop that, but by that time she walking and trying to talk, so I talk with her. And she listen and take it in, you know. I tell her about my father and I tell her about Modibe and I tell her that the woman we staying with is harsh but she mean good. She know that already, and she know the woman love her for if she did have breasts with milk, she would have did take her away from me long time. She know that this is true. She nod her head. The little girl know is true; she could see that for the woman tell her to call her "Mama".

But I also tell her things I make up as true. I tell her about my father's mother. She is one of those who come from somewhere else. Is just one time when the drums beating heavy that I see her. I see her spinning around, spinning around like dry leaf can spin by themselves when they catch up in spider's web and breeze is blowing. Just spinning with her hands spread out like wings to balance her so that she can't drop to the ground. I don't know what else happen for it was nearly morning and I was a very little girl and I sleep off. I never see my grandmother again and nobody tell me anything, so I say to myself that she spin and spin and her feet lift up off the ground and she fly to the heaven in the sky that Daddy B and all the others, whether chapel or Tabernacle or church people tell us about. I tell the little girl about that, about how my grandmother spin and spin until she lift off the ground and fly off to heaven.

You want to see the little eyes taking in all of this. And she look so much like my grandmother. Funny, for when Mass Eustace see her he always saying how she have his mother face, and so too say his rich sister that sending all this American clothes for her and you can know that they are new clothes, nobody ever wear them before. You can know it by the smell, and sometimes they still have price tag on them. The church box clothes never had no price tag on them, so you know they wear already. I was so glad for the little girl for I had no friend living with me except the fowls. I couldn't even go back to Christian Endeavour. I don't know why, but Neville would tell me all that happen. That is Neville, the boy next door. Very bright. He is going to be a teacher. If I didn't have Nothing, I would be nothing more than "Gal". But that don't matter now for I am going to be an angel whether she or I like it or not.

8. turnbury

Even as a small boy, I knew that Turnbury was nothing to be proud of, though we named Turnbury were supposed to be proud and proud of it. How many people around us carried the last name of the place where they lived! We did have two stout pillars and a sign across them saying "Turnbury", but I sensed that that was an old sign and a sign of an old time. I supposed that in that old time, there was no elephant and cutlass grass growing quite out-of-hand by the gate, that the ruts which the cart made – carriage in those days – would have been quickly filled in with stones and cemented down, and that the sign would have been painted or whatever, so that people could really see it and read it; that the stone work would have been cleaned out now and again and even whitewashed as the lesser folks did with the stones they had around their garden beds. Walking barefooted, which is how we walked most of the time, along the rutted pathway, we very often cut our ankles against the stones, and so many times that one sore stayed with us for months, opened by another stone every time one healed.

This ten-year-old supposed to be proud to be a Turnbury, and said to be proud, would come out every evening bathed but barefooted with small flies – gingy flies – swarming round my sore ankle or the bandage which tied up my sore ankle, and lean against the pillar. I never told my mother why I was there but I guess she knew, and I know that I wished my being there was our business alone, but everyone seemed to know. I could not hide. They, the district people, would pass calling out to me, "Red Ibo, you a wait for Drunkareddy," which translated meant, "Red-skinned boy, you are waiting for your drunkard of a father." And I was. And he was always drunk. I was waiting for my father, for I preferred to be the one to guide him over the stones rather than leave this job to any of those village people. And I didn't want them to have to take him the ten chains to our house because they loved to talk about our business. I hated it when one of them would say to my mother, "See me bring you parcel come. Mi find him at . . .", and name the place at which my father in his drunken stupor had fallen down. Such a person might go further and say, "Nuh jump her tonight, you know, Turnbury; you no see you send her up again already," and look at my mother's protruding stomach lifting the hem of her skirt, which even I with no dress-sense could see was not meant to be worn to bend over a wash pan of dirty clothes and soap suds but was meant for the better days of entertaining.

I know for sure from these same people that a better day had existed, for I heard talk as I walked with my sore foot on the roads: "Captain muss a turn eena him grave. Look what Doris come to! Sore foot. Doris never know nothing bout that. Mussi dat why she can't treat the pickney dem sores. Shoes everywhere she was going, although the sole never touch ground for is carriage and horse and coach man take her everywhere." So I waited to take my father from whoever brought him to the so-called gate. He would smell as if he was pickled in rum. I would hold him around the waist and lead him, though I barely reached his waist and I probably looked as if I was holding onto him for protection. And in a sense I was. I was walking in humiliation but still with a sense that the man I was leading was a protective cloak. Perhaps he saw me as some sort of vindication of his existence, for he would put his arm around my neck and thus bonded we would arrive at our front step where my mother would be waiting and would put her arms around both of us and lead us into the house.

With a turn of her head she would indicate that I could let go and go sit on the bench at the table where there was cornmeal porridge in a tin can with a handle waiting for me. She would lead him into their bedroom, coming out of which soon I would hear her giggles and hear her speaking the kind of baby talk through which she communicated with my younger sibs. She was happy with him and so was I, for his presence made our household whole. We were a total community and understandably needed every member in place. We had nothing to do with the people around. I can't even remember the name of one. They had names for us "Red Ibo" for me, "Turnbury" for my father and "Doris" for my mother. They knew us because of our history; they had no history for us to know them by. They had their school but we did not go there, so I did not sit beside or play with any of their children.

My father said, and my mother agreed, that she had more education in her thumbnail than they had in all their school, and she did teach us to read, to do sums and sing songs. I learnt that she had been to what they call high school in a place far away called Savanna-la-Mar, that she knew about all sort of things – how to make cakes and jams and things those village people never even heard about. We should have been attending the church, where my mother said our family had had what she called a "pew", for years. I had difficulty with the word "pew". "Our own bench," she said, in which only members of the family could sit. We couldn't go there, though, and I used to wonder if there was anyone to dust that bench. We didn't go because, my parents said, the church was too far from where we lived and our coach was not working. Said coach lived under a tree and had done so for as long as I could remember. If it had moved at all I would have known. We played hide and seek in it.

The one quarrel I knew my parents to have had happened like this. He was going out to where we knew he would return as usual drunk. My mother was holding his face and kissing it and talking her baby talk to him, when he pushed her away. I couldn't imagine why my mother would do that. She must know that that kind of behaviour could only happen after he came home drunk. What he said to her in his anger stayed with me.

"Get your black ass out of my way. Because that black bitch is coming here, you want me to change my behaviour. Well, not a damn of that. You can go on and continue cleaning the house as if the queen is coming here. That's your business. Just leave mine alone. Not a damn thing to make her queen except that a white man choose to marry her because her father had two coins to knock together. And while you cleaning, see if you can clean up the two copper vats that they give my people for you." My mother looked embarrassed and I was embarrassed for her. She had indeed been cleaning up and dusting, but nobody had told us that the bitch who thought herself a queen was coming to visit. The black old lady came but didn't stay long.

The first thing she did was cry. She pulled the six of us children to her bosom and, looking at my mother's extended stomach, she wept, bringing the outside into our house and to us, for she was muttering what I had heard so often on the street: "Captain must be turning in his grave. *Look at this,*" she said so often, looking at the coach, looking at the sugar works. "What a shame." My mother's face was growing red. It is when she took us aside and, talking so loudly that my mother could not but hear, said that we didn't have to live with the memory of a father whose life couldn't stand scrutiny, we should think of ourselves as our grandfather's line, that my mother's face moved from red to white. The old lady paid no attention.

She pressed on to talk about the beauties of grandfather Smith's life. "He was a judge, you know." I knew this to be an important position and that he came from Scotland. I was wondering if she too came from this illustrious place, for she was leading us to believe that she was as right as he, but did not mention where she was from and what was her claim to glory. If she had wanted to fill this gap, it would have to stay until another time, for my mother called me "Everard, son." I am usually called just "son", so I knew this was an important call. And it was. "Go and wash your foot and take your grandmother to the gate," she said. "I think that the bread man will still be around can give your grandmother a ride back home on his donkey."

Grandmother stopped speaking and my mother was able to say to her and the air, "I cannot allow you to teach my children to disrespect their father. You are my mother. Should my husband hear that you have been doing this, he might get violent with you. And could anybody blame him? Now where would that leave me? I would have to make a choice between my mother and my husband and I am not ready to do that as yet."

Grandmother and I walked to the gate and she told me of all the charms of my grandfather Smith. Of how he reared his children; even of how he gave money to the Turnburys to fix their business so that my mother could be economically comfortable with them. She told me that the house which Captain Smith had built was still there with its many beauties and that it was open to me. I could even come with her now if I had on my shoes. Shoes? Which shoes? I asked her one question. Did grandfather Smith's gate have pillars and a sign with his name on it? It did not. I heard something about "poor show great" and "all that glitters not being gold", but then and there I knew without doubt which was the more important side of the family. It was the one from whom a whole area had taken its name and the one which had a gate with its name on it. I helped my black grandmother to get onto the donkey and then stumbled to my home trying to avoid the sharp rocks which made the path to our front door. My father did not lurch in until we all had gone to bed except my mother, who I knew was worrying. I woke to hear her cooing and knew that all was well again.

My mother could not have foreseen that there were mighty forces that could stymie her plan to keep us respecting our father. The big one was death. She always either went to her mother for the delivery of her babies or had her mother come to her. With the vexation between them, she decided to leave her mother out of the equation. When her labour pains came, there was no one to call. I did what she told me to do. I boiled water, heated towels with the water and put them on her belly, but that could not stop the pain and the groaning. She had been in pain for about four hours before my father lurched in. Fortunately he was his usual drunk and therefore useless self, and had had to be brought home. Fortunately for us, I thought then, this man heard the groans and insisted on coming in, though my father was telling him to mind his own business. It was he who sent for my grandmother. While we waited, my father sat under a tree and wept. I think he wept because he realized he couldn't manage and the black bitch was coming, and with her, embarrassment at his uselessness. The black bitch came too late. The mirror they put to my mother's nose remained shine. My grandmother didn't cry this time. She started packing our few clothes.

By the time she was finished, our yard was overflowing with the inquisitive bad-minded neighbours whom my mother would have wished out of her yard. The black queen used them. This one to take a message here or there. In what seemed no time, a coffin was built and decorated and my mother's body put in it. Our clothes had been bundled and a wagon was on its way. My father came to life when they were about to put me in the wagon. "Have a heart old woman," he said to her who had been the black bitch who thought she was a queen. "What company will I have if you take Son with you too?"

The black bitch said, "A malnourished and ill child will be of no use to you. He too will soon die. Let me feed him up and I will send him back to you. Even now I will send him back at weekends to see to you. You know that I keep my word." She even went across and touched him on the arm, saying, "Take care of yourself." With that we left Turnbury.

Life was not easy with the old woman who said we should call her "Ma". The problem was order. Ma believed in order. We ate better; she attended to our sores; we had clean clothes, some she made, some she had dressmakers and tailors make. That was nice. We had beds and blankets – but the order! I could not sit and watch ants, I could not wander around as I wished, could not sleep just because I felt like it. We had to do things according to time. We had to get up, fetch water and bathe in that cold water early in the morning; we had to rush off to school and not leave for home until a bell was rung. We had to go to church at a certain time and not leave until everybody was ready to leave and we had to sit with books at certain times in the day, spelling and figuring. I was luckier than the others. At school they said I was too old and big for the class in which my level of knowledge prepared me to sit. I didn't have to go to school as such, but Ma apprenticed me to a plant chemist and I had to be with him at certain times of the day, carrying instruments for him, watching as he tested this pan of sugar and the other, lifting them and sometimes reading the tester. He told Ma that I had a head for those things. Ma got me a horse and I was now to go outside of the area and as far sometimes as where the sea met the land, to work with the chemist.

This man, the chemist Mr Suarez, looked more like my father than like Ma and I was now meeting more people who looked like me and like him, and having people call me by my name, Everard, instead of Red Ibo. Ma did not allow me to forsake my father. She had to keep her word, she said, so every weekend found me away from my brothers and sisters and on my way back to Turnbury to be with him. He had not changed. He was still drunk and taken home at night by just anybody. The house had changed, though. It was like a rubbish heap. There was no order at all. You could find a pot in the bed, dirty, for my father had cooked and instead of turning the food out into a plate, had taken the pot to bed with him and left it right there when he went off to his work as a drunk. I made it my business to tidy the house at weekends.

This is how I realized that bits of furniture were missing. Sometimes even a window was missing. Without the money my mother was giving him from what, I later discovered, was left to her personally in a bank account by her father, my father was selling off bits of furniture and of the house to pay for his alcohol. And people were so unkind that they let him do this. I don't know if I am being unreasonable but I do think that it would have been better if one or some of them had given my father a good hiding and told him to shape up rather than to condone his drinking and have him destroy our heritage. This is when I decided that my father was too much for me to fight. I was earning and saving. I could save better than Ma. I put my father in a retirement home. Let them tar his hide and fight with him.

Some people have bones in the back of their body which keep them standing firm. My father had rum in his. The old people's home run by the church to which his fathers were, he had said, attached, would of course not allow him to drink. He curled up like a snail and died. In memory of the old Turnbury who had once been one of the pillars of the church, or out of respect for his colour, I don't know which one, they buried him in their churchyard. A year later I had enough money to give him a headstone and that I did. Not a tomb. Just a headstone. He had been buried as a charity case so he was put way in the back, in an almost inaccessible place. Exit Samuel Turnbury. Indeed the Turnburys. For I was the only one of us conceived in rum who attended his little service and was at the installation of his headstone.

My colour and my training kept me in the company of brown and white people. I even had connections with Americans who were coming around and trying to set up businesses in which they would buy green bananas in Jamaica and ship them to their homeland in the north. By the time the bananas arrived, they would be ready to be sold as ripe bananas. The black people had been planting bananas for years; they needed to plant more commercially and plant the types the Americans needed. I could get the suckers from my friends in the neighbouring parishes and this I did. My business now was to get the black people to do what I wished. I didn't have much connection with them and there was not much love lost between me and them. I could not forget the teasing from them at Turnbury. It would be good if I could go and plant at Turnbury, but who would do the clearing and planting? Though I did have land at Turnbury, this was the last place I wished to go and put down even one root of banana or anything else. It is just plain good luck that took me to Sturge Town and to Mr Eustace Reid.

I must give myself the credit: it was not just good luck. It is something I planned and I still cannot believe how wise I was. I knew that the black people controlled the banana planting business. I knew that they were crucial to my success as a marketer but I was very aware that I had yet to find the knack of communicating with them. I fancied that I would find them at Brown's Town market: everyone came there. I was looking for someone who was not totally comfortable with his business and was willing to think about a change. Mr Reid was there with bananas among other things. Here was a possibility. He was one of the few males selling in the market. I thought through that. Mr Reid would prefer to do his marketing in a different way. I struck up a conversation with him. It wasn't difficult. Mr Reid had moved around white and non-black men of all kinds. He had been in Clarendon and worked closely with white bushas and owners, and in addition the Indians who were settling in there in significant numbers.

You could see he was a hard-working man, not given to insolence nor uppitiness, and that he was likely to have got on well with the non-black master class and even got backlands to buy from them. He looked too like he would be from a family that had travelled even if he himself had not. My guesses were right on all scores, but the right and deciding guess was that Mr Reid did not feel that he should be sitting down in a market selling; he really should have a wife to do this but either could not find one or the one he had was not willing to come to the market. Mr Reid was willing to let me sell all his bananas for him and have me take a percentage of the profit for my labours. I agreed to visit him and found a very tidy farm with land space yet to be used. Mr Reid would consider putting this unused space into bananas but couldn't seriously consider this for he had a labour problem. I let him see that this was no problem, for I was willing to make my hands dirty. In this way I got my first client and a plot of land on which to grow bananas commercially.

Mr Reid and I got on well. He was always willing to move over and give me space. He acceded to my suggestion, for instance, about buying a dray and mule and letting me pay for it with my labour. But I didn't understand his home situation. There were three women there. There was Lily, the meek and mild, and Miss Maud, the she-dragon whom I imagined preferred to labour on the farm rather than take produce to the market. Then there was the young woman so slim you could hardly see her. This was the apple of his eye and whatever the relationship he had with her, she was bound to be his heir. I gave Mr Reid's situation further thought and came to the conclusion that I could get it all by becoming a part of the family through the girl. She really was not much to look at and she was black – didn't my grandfather, the judge, marry my grandmother, the "black bitch"? How could her colour be a problem? What really attracted me about her was that she could do all the things that I had only heard that my mother could do. I would watch her preparing guavas to make jams and jellies or dicing coconut for coconut cake and be vexed on behalf of my mother, who was a brown woman and had learnt all these skills and didn't get a chance to practise them. It seemed that something was wrong with the world if this could be so. But what was really wrong was the resentment I had against the little nothing of a girl. I wanted to defile her for my mother's sake.

Mr Reid died. Mysteriously. And here was my opportunity to get at the girl for her father's land and to debase her. I did quite well with this goal. I managed to move into the house. I could make my move soon from this vantage point. The she-dragon played into my hands. She caught me watching the girl as she worked at a piece of embroidery. My high-coloured mother could have done this that this skinny black girl was doing so confidently, I was thinking as I stared at her, but didn't get a chance. My mother even went to school to do this kind of thing, yet she never had a chance. The she-dragon saw something else in my eyes and thought I had a man's interest in the girl. She virtually proposed marriage, and I accepted. This was an excellent point from which to carry out my plan. Just the place: marriage. Wasn't this where my mother had found debasement? I should have taken the girl away to effect this. There was no privacy in the house. Trying to assert my bridegroom rights, with the girl struggling and screaming, the she-dragon came in and dragged me off of her.

I had done so very well for the people in the village: they were planting bananas commercially and I was helping them to rake in more money than they had ever seen. Through me they were accessing the trappings of a middle-class life, a life I as a brown man ought to have been exposed to but didn't see, until after age twelve when I went to live with my black grandmother. They now had tallboys and all kinds of chests of drawers in their house. Some had sewing machines, and the little sugar mill for juicing cane and making sugar for domestic use was common in the area because

I was willing to source it for them. Yet when the dragon and I fell out over the girl, nobody came to my side. It felt like Turnbury all over again: black people unsympathetic to my cause because I was a brown man – "red", as they prefer to say.

When the other dragon came from Panama, it became crystal clear to me that I had lost out again; I couldn't beat the black people. This is a fact that I have to live with. The other that I wish I didn't have to live with is my malice towards the girl. It forced me to think, though. My father once made a comment which suggested that he felt my mother was forced on him because she could bring to Turnbury some material things it needed. If this was my father's psychological path, his path to drunkenness, then my projected relationship with the girl was just a reliving of my father's relationship, and the subsequent shame or whatever power had driven him to the bottle. I was forced in my meditation to consider myself lucky that the two dragons had intervened. Without that, I would have ended up drunk somewhere trying to deal with malice towards the person in my bed. And it could happen again, for there were other up-and-coming black men with daughters. I could not allow this to be my path. Its possibility is what took me to the church in Brown's Town.

I can't say I had known Reverend Henderson. I had of course seen him but didn't know who he was. He was a head above everyone in height and a regular at the market. You could not help seeing him. The thing is, you could not know he was a reverend unless someone told you or you heard somebody addressing him, for he looked so ordinary. I had never seen him in the whole heap of clothes and jewellery worn by those at the church to which my grandmother sent us. He did not look like God had sent him down here for a brief time to judge sinners; he looked as if he belonged on earth and had known sin and had dealt with it. The black parsons were now many; the Rev even had a black assistant. But he, I was glad to see, was a white man; I could relate to him. I made an appointment and within a week we were talking. I told him about my sinful thought and plan and what nearly happened. I told him about my mother and father – I was so relieved to get that off my chest.

There was no surprise on his face that could make me feel like the biggest sinner in the world with the craziest parents ever. He just said that every place has its particular sin and that Jamaica's was race and colour prejudice and the attendant exploitation of black women. That made me feel almost normal. "That doesn't mean," he continued, "that it has to go on like this. And the good thing here is that you know it. You know that what you have been feeling and doing and what your father did was wrong and you would like it to end. That is why you are here." So I am good enough! "What is lacking from your life is real companionship," he said, and invited me to attend his church.

I got myself a Bible and I attended, even to Sunday School. There you got passages that you are to read. I dutifully read them every night. Being in the church did not bring the spirit of the Lord upon me; I was the same Everard Turnbury that had spoken to Reverend Henderson. Most of the passages I didn't even understand. But I was reading; I was recognizing words. The substance behind the words came when in Sunday School people argued about meaning. I got a good deal too when the reverend preached, for what he tended to do was to explain the scriptures. In time my word recognition got so good that I could go behind the words to some kind of meaning and join in the discussion in the Sunday School. I hadn't known before that I was susceptible to black people's taunts because I saw myself as inferior, as the "red man", the intellectually dim. With my new reading skills, I changed my sense of myself. I was now a brown man. If anyone called out to me as "Red Ibo", I wouldn't turn around. I knew, though, that I could not totally heal myself until I had done something for the girl. I was not brave enough to go back there and ask her pardon and claim her as my proper wife. I didn't really feel for her. To go back as her husband I knew was wrong and could only lead to my exploitation of her, but if I could help in any way to make her economic life a little easier, I would. When I heard she was in business I went and offered myself. The foreign cousin, or whoever she was, with children nearly as "red" as I, one in her arms and the other holding on to the hem of her skirt, made me know that with my colour, I couldn't help them. Colour again, but it wasn't me this time. They would have to go to the foot of the cross on their own to see if they could justify their prejudice against me. What I did was to acknowledge legally that the girl was my wife and should come into whatever I left on this earth. What more could I do?

It was I penning this, who had not yet quite worked out my relationship with Cousin Nothing, the material beneficiary of Everard Turnbury's turnaround. Still, while I was smoothing out his mini mat to put it in place on Nothing's master mat, I was thinking, why was he here? He was only Nothing's first husband. No kin to me, who was yet not quite sure how Nothing was related to me. Then light struck. After all I was brought up in England, "God save our gracious Queen" and all that. Surely I could be gracious. I knew "gracious". And didn't I inherit from him? Curiosity took me past graciousness. What was the nature of the family structure out of which this white man, Everard's father, came and did it conduce to drinking so foolishly? I had some time ago come across a record – a commission of inquiry, I think – in which it had been said that Europeans imported for labour here found the climate difficult, ended up straying from the plantations and falling down drunk in gutters in the city. Was Everard's father one of those imported to be used as labour and had he taken up the habit of drinking because the physical environment was spitting him out? I walked all the way to the town in which the old people's home lay, in which Everard's father had passed his last days, to begin my research on that family. It appears that Everard had either not tombed his father or the bushes had so grown over that stone that I could not find it. I could find no monument to him in the churchyard. I found a Turnbury in the register of the home, though. It was Samuel. This couldn't be a coincidence, I said. Everard's father's name is Samuel. The house in which I live, the land which I have inherited belonged to Samuel Turnbury.

Further confirmation came when I unrolled some papers knotted in cloth. Must have been Doris's work. Here I found baptism certificates for her children and herself and even for Everard. His father was listed as Samuel and listed as born in England. I went to the christening records in Spanish Town and found an Alston Turnbury as the father of Samuel, he too being born in England, and I saw there that Samuel was baptized at age seven. I found in yet another place that there were but twelve years between the ages of Alston and Samuel. Perhaps not a father and son relationship at all. My "little grey cells" started to work, as my favourite Agatha Christie detective would say. I had read how people had been press-ganged in England into coming to the West Indies. I could see this teenager Alston and the little boy Samuel, kidnapped, blindfolded and thrown into the hold of a ship and not released until they could feel the rolling of the ship over the water. I had even read of a little girl – a native – being sold in a market in England. My emotions were engaged. I was feeling as sorry for them as I was for those blacks making the middle passage. As I fought with being sorry for these white men, I told myself that I was just making up a story. Then I thought to myself, *If this is not even the story of the Turnburys, it is that of some other white people in this country*, and gave myself permission to be sorry for them. How did they manage to get this twenty-acre estate which they had treated so shabbily? This was hard work but I did it. I checked the records in Kingston and Spanish Town and found out that this twenty-acre plot had been cut off from a four-hundred-acre estate that had belonged to Major Turnbury and given as a gift to Alston and Samuel Turnbury. The records showed no wife for Major Turnbury, nor was he listed in any clubs or societies or at any social event. Quite a recluse this major was. I would have left it at that and my nasty mind would not have had a chance to speculate, if the resident seer had not backed me up on a spot on the road and told me that the place I was living in did not like women, that the one woman who had tried to live there had died in childbirth and that God had cursed it because of the major's sodomy. Dirty mind said, *Aha, these two young men captured in England and imported into Jamaica had been the major's playthings and been rewarded with land*. Indeed the title was in both names – Alston and Samuel. I couldn't meet them in the flesh, but I did meet Everard.

I could fully appreciate the village scorn which the two lonely young white people must have felt throughout their lives. One had chanced to look at Captain Smith's daughter and got himself pinned into what he could not manage. I doubt that the seer was even living in the area at the time, but whether he was or not, the vibrant village memory would have telescoped this word to him. What a pity that the village could not have been more supportive. It struck me that what might have befallen these young men could be part of the black history as well. I didn't feel any need to put Alston or Samuel in the mat. But the mess stayed with me translating into the question, What was I going to do with this anti-woman place? I shelved the issue and told myself that I would go right back to work, dealing with those I knew were my kin, putting my American aunt and uncle in the mat.

part 3.

9. john and sally

I saw John and Sally as the two-faced god Janus or as Siamese twins, for their names were always twinned. Herbert got Christmas cards from them every year signed *John and Sally* and in a bracket after that, *your brother and sister*. In a new line there was *P.S. Give our love to Polly.* Aunt Polly – Pauline – did not get a card. Perhaps they saw my father and his sister as they saw themselves – as one.

Once sometime during the year a photograph came in an envelope from John and Sally to Herbert and Pauline beginning a long photograph trail. There were a man and a woman in the picture and two very happy children in short pants. I was pleased to see not just the smiling faces of these girls, but their hair! Though they were black like me, their hair touched their shoulders. It was straight and curled like Little Miss Muffet's.

Aunt Polly turned up her nose. "Don't they know that those girls are too young to have their hair straightened? They are giving these children all sorts of complexes as well as endangering their physical health."

The lady in the picture did not resemble the man. Aunt Polly said that was not Sally, but John's wife. I hardly heard her. I was concentrating on her hair.

"Look, Aunt Polly, look at her hair." Said hair was hanging across her cheek and dropping down where her breast should be. "They got the hair from her, Aunt Polly," I was saying, glad that this newcomer to the family had brought long hair with her.

"That is bought hair, my dear. That is a wig," Aunt Polly said.

This was the first time that I heard of people wearing wigs outside of a play. And black people at that.

Another time Herbert and Pauline got a letter from John and Sally and there was a photograph in it but of only one person. You could hardly see whether this was a man or a woman, for the person had on what I was informed was a mortar board and a long garment such as the priests wear in my church. The writing on the back said, *Me at graduation. Your sister, Sally Beaufort MA.*

Aunt Polly said, "So Sally married. And she have a master's degree. Good. Wonder why she don't send us a picture of her wedding and of her children?"

Not long after, there was another letter from John and Sally with another photograph. This time there were, as with the first, a man and a woman and two children. The man's hair was sleek and shiny.

Aunt Polly's nose wrinkled. "Oh my God. Him conk him hair." What was "conk"? She described the process of putting a harsh liquid called lye in your hair to make it straight and wondered if they conked the boy's hair too, for we could guess from the fact that one of the children was in trousers long enough to be seen at the ankles and the other in dress that one was a boy and the other a girl. As in the picture which Sally and John had sent of Sally alone, the children were wearing mortar boards and long gowns. The writing at the back explained, *Henry and I at the children's graduation from prep school.* I was glad for this explanation for I considered myself to be quite bright. My parents and my teachers thought so too. How was I to see myself if these children, no older than I, were already graduating from college.

The truth is they did graduate before me, Sally's two as well as John's two, and the photographs came more regularly of one or another of them pictured at work – *the first Negro to hold this position.* There is a round table in our hall which holds photographs. It is full of proud people who had burst the tape in America and were "the first Negroes" to do this or that. I was related to all of them. There was a similar table in my grandparents' home in Jamaica similarly stacked with these tape-bursting relatives of mine. The most recent of the pictures on both tables had a beautiful face with hair all around it like a halo. This was Joy, John's daughter, formerly one of the two long-haired. Joy was teaching at Howard University away from her home in Virginia. John and Sally wanted their mother to see whether someone had "done something" to her and to pray for her, for she was getting in trouble with the police by preaching about blackness. Bully for her. I was glad of an opportunity to lecture these old people about the condition of blacks in the world and about Martin Luther King and Malcolm X. They couldn't understand why Joy, who was a Jamaican, should get herself involved in that. She should come home to them. They were shocked to know that America was her home. I took Sally and John's address, wrote introducing myself, and asked for Joy's address. A fruitful correspondence developed between us, allowing me now to create the mini mat of that part of the family. I would make only one – the John and Sally mini mat.

Joy was really seriously into Black Power. She sent me copies of talks she had given and newspaper clippings of reports on her addresses. I asked her why she was so involved, just because I wanted to know more about her and could think of no other question. I got the whole story in what read like fiction – a short story. First of all she wanted me and anybody else who cared to know that she was not into Black Power so that a black boy could marry a white girl, though this is where it had started. John the second was really her cousin, as I knew, but was more than a cousin for her emotionally. Their parents, John and Sally, had always found apartments in the same building so that the children grew up like brothers and sisters. I could see that, for I understood that John the second was not the son of John the first but his nephew. They all went to college at Hampton. If John the second had wanted to marry out of the Negro race, he could have chosen any of many fine Native Indian girls, for they were in abundance at Hampton, Joy offered. Instead he had to go and court this blonde girl and win her – but not her parents, her story went. I knew a part of that story. The wedding picture had come. There was this black boy in a suit that made him look like a pelican or penguin and this slim white girl, a bit of brown hair escaping from her white veil, she looking for all the world like a female Jesus. You expected to look farther down her form and see an open heart. My mother had put this picture in front of all the others muttering that "this was real people" and she didn't know why "some others" that she could name couldn't read the clock, see "what o'clock a strike", "straighten her hair and get a good job in a store".

Joy was saying that this marriage had brought problems not only to John the second but to the whole family, for they felt for each other. They never knew when he would come home a dead bag of bones. It was John the second's arrest for careless driving that made Joy decide to deepen her relationship with the political organization in Washington. The guy was not even driving when he was arrested; he was merely waiting by the elementary school for his wife, who was teaching there. What an embarrassment to her and to him, and a scare for the children and the teachers, to see him handcuffed and pushed down by the head into a police car. He was driven away to the police station and charged with careless driving and resisting arrest and put in the newspaper as such. Perhaps, she said, if John the second had not been her brother-cousin she could have left the whole business behind, but he was. And though she was angry that his marriage choice had brought nervousness and tension to the family, that the police and other white people did not approve of his marriage choice was no reason for them to harass him. In any case, if the marriage stuck and produced children they would be black children and suffer the lot of black people, so she had to give some of her life to making their path straight. John the second and his white wife left the area for the north and the family had some peace, but Joy didn't stop agitating and getting herself quoted and bringing more fear to the family. They needn't fear, she said, for she was well covered by the organization and they had attracted some sound lawyers.

Her sister, the other one of the long straightened hair, was, she said, a blessing to her family. She, Grace, didn't have a political thought in her head. She had married an "Old Tom" who loved the fact that her straightened hair could brush against her back, who loved America as it was, who had bought an apartment building which he refused to rent to blacks for they were careless and untidy, and who could not understand why these black people couldn't all raise themselves up by their boot straps as he had done. John the second's sister, the other child of Sally, was making her way up the ranks of a school and expected in a few years to be the head of a school. The first Negro woman . . . . None of these needed the scandal of having a revolutionary sister-cousin, so she now rarely went home and seemed to be getting the collection of photographs sent to my grandparents and my father and aunt. I imagined another round table in the centre of Joy's living room with the same set of photographs of black people who had burst the American tape and were the "first Negroes to . . .". As I read her story I could not but remember my own brother, Evan, who was where there was no round table, who could not escape to the North, and of whom we hardly spoke at home, for it was "not my business", my parents said; my business was to "thrive" and nobody can say I didn't. My "thriving" was for my brother and myself. I knew her pain.

My house was new to me and I new to it. I had done my bachelor's in Jamaica and gone back home, to come back to walk at graduation. Blessed Nothing had chosen to die about that time, so I could get her feet ready for her coffin without having to change my airline ticket. I had hardly returned home before the letter came, sent on by my grandparents, that I had got a university award which allowed me to do postgraduate studies there in Jamaica. The only person who thought going back to take it up was unfortunate was the fellow who had started gazing at me again. I took my body out of his line of vision and went back. By then I knew that I was landed, but was more tickled by the thought than the reality.

It was only after postgraduate work was successfully completed and I had accepted the little low-paying job as an instructor that I realized being landed meant paying taxes and that my grandfather had been taking care of all of this while I studied. Now that I was finished with all that and was earning, he thought it was time for me to get serious about my real estate. He took me to the property and shook his head at the state of it. I was undaunted. The course I was teaching was boring me and, I suppose, the students, for I was getting no energy from them. Here, though, was life and a challenge. Neville shrugged his ancient shoulders and left my decision to me. If Euphemia could go to Panama and chop down bush and set up business, why couldn't I.

The house was what they call a stone nog. That's the only reason it was still standing. A wooden house would have been more romantic but it would not have waited for me to decide to be an owner before it crumbled. The small veranda had wooden shutters and a tiled floor. I decided that this would be my space and I felt that I had made the right move after the seer informed me that the house didn't like women: it was wise for me to stay on the veranda and slowly and tenderly seduce the rest of the house. Things began to happen early on. If I hadn't seen Derek Walcott's *Ti Jean* dramatized and seen the bolom going from house to house and crying, I probably would not have heard it. There was this everlasting, every-night crying of a child or children – and hadn't a baby died in this house as the seer had told me?

There was too a constant ping on the top of the house as if small stones were landing on it. As this happened in the day, I paid no attention to it. It was the baby or babies crying in the night that destabilized me. I mightn't have a rod and a staff but I did have a mat and a cutlass. As soon as the crying started I would put the mat over my head so that it fell all over me. "Thou anointest my head with oil; my cup runneth over": I don't know if I was trying for this, using the mat to represent oil. I wish I could say that the crying stopped immediately. It was as loud and as piercing as ever even with my mat flowing over me. What my action did do was to get me to think of all these relatives that Nothing and I had sewn together and to think of what each would have done in this situation or advised me to do. It was in this mode that I came to regret that Miss Cookie had not been sewn into the mat. How could I have been so careless, when she had told me so many stories, one of which came forcefully to my mind? It was one of these tales of origin that get so little attention in the study of the region's orature. This one related to puss and dog.

For whatever reason, God had made it so that the whole public could see the lovemaking and reproduction exercises of dogs. Cat thought that God had intended Dog to be the laughingstock of the world and had accordingly berated Dog caught in this twisted and compromising position and duly laughed, whereupon God cursed Cat, saying: "You will do your thing in private but everybody will know what you are doing." So cats, Miss Cookie concluded, are forced to scream and carry on when they are making love.

Could this be it? I had my cutlass, my water boots, my flashlight and my courage. I followed the sound further in the bush this time. The woeful screaming did stop as I got closer and I did see cats but saw no out-of-order behaviour. I gave thanks that it stopped if only for a while and judged that if my presence could have this effect on the sound, perhaps there was something to the tale of origin and the noise was indeed coming from courting cats. I would control them further, and even if they did not stop the noise, at least I would be sure what was making that noise. I set milk in discarded tins around the house and sure enough, after that the cats and their caterwauling were right around my house. I calmed myself with the understanding that everything has its mating season and that cats must have theirs too. I was to have several little kittens about five weeks after. Their presumptuous mothers thought they, not I, had been left this property by Nothing and Everard, and took over the house.

10. the home

It was not just the pinging on the roof that had been a bother to my senses. Along with them had been these mighty gallops like the devil and his friends having chariot races. Soon this was less and the half-eaten bodies of rats as large as the cats, sunning themselves like tourists on a beach but giving off a mighty stench, were everywhere. It was not a pleasant sight or smell but at least I now knew that it was not the devil in my roof nor unchristened babies weeping around me and asking me to help them to get into purgatory. It was left now for me to advise the cats that it was I who was paying the taxes on the house and that nobody was paying me to tidy up behind them. This was how I was forced to move beyond the veranda and claim more space.

I found my wood. All the floors were wood except for the veranda where I had been camping. It was about this time that my interaction with the villagers began. I had been for walks and I had been to the shop, so everyone knew me. Who had not met me on the road or in the shop certainly had met those who had, and I was the new thing, the news, so I was well known. It was still only the seer who was brave enough to engage me in conversation. He must have been checking up on me, for he knew about the cats and about the rats. He also knew that I couldn't manage the floors, nay, told me that I couldn't manage the floors and that he would get me a helper.

"Not everyone will come, you know," he warned me, "for everyone know that is a haunted house you have and that it don't like women. But Miss," he added to my surprise and joy, "you have something there can counteract them. That's why you are there so long. Once people know that you have your own powers they will stop being afraid of your place. You are going to be frightened at how much respect they will have for you."

He was right. Miss Merci and her daughters came to work on a task basis and cleaned the house from top to bottom. Then she arranged for Clair, the eldest, to come to me twice weekly to keep things in order. The young man who was speaking to her was Timothy and he was a goodish carpenter. He fixed the roof of one of the bedrooms and replaced an absent window and I moved into that with the mat, only entertaining on the veranda now. Once Clair couldn't come for a week and she sent a friend of hers to work in her place. I lost a pair of earrings that week. I am careless and likely to take off my earrings and leave them anywhere that I have been sitting, reading. Since I always wear earrings, I usually know pretty early that I have misplaced them and right away begin the search, usually with success. I knew when Clair's friend Sasha was about to leave, what had happened and began retracing my steps. No earrings.

Then I heard a thud. Somebody had fallen in my room. There was a cry and I went to investigate. Sasha was on the floor. It seems that a sprig from her shoe had caught in the mat by my bedside and tripped her, but more important than that for me, my earrings were shining on the floor close by. Sasha apparently had had them in her breast pocket and with the fall they had been flung out. I took in the situation and simply said, "This is not an ordinary mat, dear." There were holes in the mat. Naturally. It is made up of joined circles so it would have circular holes in it. Neither my feet nor my shoes, nor those of Clair, ever got caught in any of these holes. Nor did Miss Merci ever suffer from them.

Somebody else got caught, though. I was taking milk from this man – Mr Honigman. Actually it wasn't from Mr Honigman himself but from one of his serfs sent out to sell his milk. I needed milk for my many cats and for my helpers, whom I had noticed took cow's milk in their mid-morning tea, though it was bush tea normally taken with just sugar. It wasn't even any great deal of milk, just a pint. I am not unattractive, I am not walking with a stick, my speech is what passes as "refined", I am not pregnant, don't wear a wedding band or have a husband at home, and there is no regular visitor. It is not surprising that some men would hear about me, ask questions and get the answers and find their way to my veranda.

Mr Honigman came to see whether I was pleased with his milk. He had known this house to be dilapidated and rundown and he was full of encomiums on what I had done to it. Could he look around? I was myself pleased with what I had done and was sucked in. I don't know if it was because I had told Mr Honigman that I would soon be taking less milk as the kittens were growing and now ready for fish and other hard foods that Mr Honigman felt he had to rush. We had hardly reached my bedroom before the man started to wheeze and apparently have ideas about what could happen in my bed. With that came the grabbing and pulling, and I am not that big to fight off Mr Bulky Honigman. The mat took over. I don't know whether he too had a loose nail in the bottom of his shoe but I do know that bragadaps Mr Honigman was on the floor and I was making my way back to the veranda.

With me in my own house in Jamaica, Herbert remembered that he had aging parents there and wondered whether he could give up waiting for Evan for two weeks and visit us. He planned to come and I planned to impress with not just the beauty of my house but the fruitfulness of my farm and to cheer him up and take his mind for a couple hours off his incarcerated heir.

Tiefing Sasha was a great help to me. Since she knew the power of my mat, I thought she was the best person to recruit for me. She brought her young man Jeremiah to help me put my farm in order. My first question to him was if Sasha had told him about my mat. She had. He knew that Sasha's fingers were a bit light but his weren't, so he didn't suppose that the mat would bother him too much. He wanted the job. Jeremiah brought along his goats to spend the time with him, eating some of the grass which he should be chopping down with his cutlass. That taught me a lesson: I could get some goats and have them keep the land cropped while giving me milk with which to feed the cats, and, if the helpers would accept it, milk for their tea.

Jeremiah suggested that he look after the goats for me. I know when I don't know, and I knew nothing about mating, certainly not of animals. Under Jeremiah's hand my flock grew; he knew when to put them to a rammy and knew where to find one and how much should be paid for the service. Jeremiah had a grass cutter. Under his hand, the land was cleared, the blanket of green parasites lifted away and I could now see that I had sugar canes and several fruit trees. I had star apples, I had mango, I had june plums, I had oranges. All were well developed, so although I was learning that a goat's bite is poisonous and likely to kill plants, as Jeremiah told me, this applied only to new plants. I could see this myself, for how could a goat bite a developed star apple tree? I carried my European sense of parks with me and saw how I could establish one.

I felt it necessary to drive home to Sasha and Jeremiah, and any other person who needed to know it, the fact that my mat was all-seeing and all-knowing and a great punisher. It was not unusual to see me walking in my yard, robed in the mat. Sometimes it began at my head and fell over my shoulders. At other times it began at the shoulders. The holes in it made it possible for me to put a belt or a thick ribbon through it and secure it around me, leaving my arms free for labour. I can tell you, the mosquitoes did not like my mat and stayed away from me. I goaded Jeremiah into planting a part of my lawn in the pattern of my mat. He used some short shrubs which looked delightful when trimmed. The whole presentation looked like a maze except that we used circles rather than squares. In the middle of this was a stone bench. The bench could hold as many as three people, but since I was the only occupant of that house, it was usually just me sitting in the middle of the green maze with my mat around my shoulders or falling from my head.

I felt as if my mat was a coat of mail and I have no doubt that Sasha and Jeremiah saw it like that. I could open my whole house to them and throw my little cash all over the place: I knew that none would be stolen. Then came the chickens. I had a car and no desire to be changing tyres, so the driveway with its sharp stones had to be transformed. I gave it a base with large stones, then, as Macadam would have done, I threw smaller stones on it. Weeds will grow even in stones, so it was my Saturday morning chore to pull weeds from my driveway. In the process I saw something that looked like a crayfish or small lobster, and there was Jeremiah screaming behind me, "Don't touch it, Miss." That was the centipede called in these parts "the forty-leg". It was supposed to be dangerous. Jeremiah advised me that where there is stone there will be forty-legs. I would have to spray constantly to kill them. Now these deadly sprays I do not like. Somewhere in the Bible it says that if you build a pit for somebody you might be the one who falls in it. I felt that way about poisons; they could as easily kill you, the human who set the poison, I thought, as kill the forty-legs or the roaches. Jeremiah offered that "The only other thing, Miss, is for you to get fowls. They beat up the forty-legs and eat them." He did call me one day to see a triumphing fowl from my neighbour's collection bashing the forty-leg against a stone. I was convinced. Moreover I was feeling a little guilty for not having on my farm, enjoying what there was to enjoy, my guardians of the non-human world, the chicken. "But," added Jeremiah, "just like how you see them scratching the soil and the stones to take out the forty-leg or the roach is the same way they scratch away at your yam hill and even peck the growing yams. They will also pick the blossoms off the peas and you won't get any." How to handle this? "Why are they doing this?" I asked.

Jeremiah said that is how they feed themselves; that fowls are self-feeding beings.

"Suppose I were to feed them. Would they eat that food and leave the one in the farm?"

"Perhaps," my gardener said, "for nearly anything can be trained."

I would get special feeding for my fowls and hope that they would not lose their instinct for ferreting out and eating forty-legs.

I fed my fowls in the maze. Me sitting usually in the rising sun and they about me. I know it is blasphemous but I say it all the same. Every morning as I fed my fowls I felt like the Jesus in the pictures, staff in hand and his sheep around him. Me and my fowls had this interaction twice daily: at sunrise and at sunset. I bought corn for them and Sasha told me I could cut up dry coconut for them. That was challenging. After she had cracked the coconuts, I still had to, with a knife, take the nut out of its shell. This is an art I never felt I mastered and I was daily in fear of the knife slipping and making for my wrist. I insisted on doing it, though, for in no aspect of my work did I want Sasha and her Jeremiah, nor even Miss Merci and Clair, who were really good people, to think that they were indispensable. Dicing the coconut was easy after that. But after all this effort, I found that the fowls were reluctant to eat, waiting I think for the corn, which I buy from the store. I set Jeremiah to plant some corn specifically for my fowls. That worked.

Joy and I had kept up our correspondence. And I was now on the receiving end of photographs of our relatives, but I had no round centre table. In any case I found the articles Joy sent more to my taste than photographs and kept a file with them. So this file was really my centre table but it only held data on Joy. Joy was writing for *Essence*. She would send me the issues. There was where I saw corn rows. I had had my hair out like hers but there was no halo look on me. Mine was an uneven frizz like Aunt Polly's. Guess the difference was in the hair type. But the corn row with the hair neatly twisted in looked more like me.

Sasha saw me looking at the models in the magazine and let me know that she did that kind of thing to white women's hair down in Ocho Rios, not far away. I let her into my hair on the understanding that she would fix it to look like my mat. The girl is gifted. And lucky too, for my colleagues loved my hair and they too wanted their hair done in that way. This provided me with a little problem, for I liked to think of my mat, my hair and my maze as my particular armorial bearing. Sasha could manage, though: the others' were never ever just like mine. She could vary the patterns so that each person had her own style. And she could remember what she had done the last time so that each person became associated with a style. She was allowed to use my veranda, with the result that my supposedly haunted house became quite a social space. The sound of stones on the roof still continued but not as something to fear, for one of my guests told me that her grandmother's house was always doing that; it had something to do with the sun and a roof that like mine is of zinc. That was good enough to quiet my fears, which fears were only in the day when I was alone, so it was not more than one on a one-to-ten scale of fear.

The big fear was that the house could harm people involved in purely female activities such as childbirth. If the cat's frequent litters were any test of femaleness, the hex on women was off. I was a source of cats. Finally I selected the two that I found most beautiful. I kept these and took the rest to the Society for the Prevention of Cruelty to Animals. A more frightening test faced me. Joy was coming to visit and, guess what, she was coming mainly because she was pregnant, had chosen not to marry and wanted to keep her baby. The plan was that she would have it here, register it in my name as mother, then adopt it and take it back with her to the States. It was while she was here that Herbert came and that old man Turnbury chose to accept my invitation to come and see what the place now looked like.

11. joy

I postponed my tutorial and went to collect my cousin from the airport. I had had pictures of Joy as a big woman but these were just visa-sized photographs under which her articles in *Essence* or *Ebony* were placed. And they were always that same one shot. You could see that her hair was soul but there was nothing else very distinctive. I had sent her a full picture of myself with my hair corn-rowed. She knew me. I did not know this aristocratic-looking woman who rushed with open arms to me after she exited the terminal. Joy was very, very light-skinned. I remembered the story of how grandmother had reportedly used Everard's colour to turn down his offer of help with the business, and I wondered what colour must her first husband have been for her to produce such a fair-skinned grandchild, and how could she have a light-skinned husband and at the same time think of people like Everard as our enemy. Pearl would have to answer this question. In time. Of course I did not know Joy's mother but I did know from my understanding of the American society and from Joy's report concerning the troubles of her cousin-brother, John, that she was not likely to be so white as to by herself have given Joy this colour. For now my main worry was having a pregnant woman in a house that supposedly did not like women. The one thing I knew was that she wouldn't be told about the house by me until I thought her system could manage this. I could not forget Keith and how his mother's cravings while he was in the womb turned him into a dasheen. Pregnancy was such a delicate thing!

I shelved my worries and my wonders and did the right thing. I took my cousin to see her grandmother and to eat the repast that was waiting for us. Pearl was beside herself. Even in tears. I felt a little snubbed. I had never had a greeting like this from her. Of course she had never seen this grandchild before. Never even seen John, the child's father, since he and his sister went to their father in their twenties. This eighty-odd-year-old woman thought she could convince Joy to stay with her. I looked at Joy. I didn't know if she had been in touch with her grandmother and confessed her pregnancy to her but I certainly had not told them anything about it. Joy looked at me and saw that I had not told them and said she didn't think she would stay but would visit often.

Then grandmother Pearl did the stupid thing born of jealousy. "How could you give up the offer to stay in this nice house with a full-time helper and hot water, air conditioner, all the things you are accustomed to in America, to live with your cousin in her old haunted wooden house!" Joy smiled but didn't answer.

It was later in our life that I realized that even if Joy had been tempted to stay with Pearl and Neville before the talk of my house, she could not resist my wooden haunted house. Joy had come to me to experience on her behalf, and on behalf of her unborn baby, all that she had read about Jamaica, and that of course is rural Jamaica. She wanted to be shut in for the nine days after the baby's birth; she wanted him or her bathed in a pan with a silver money in it; she wanted to drink (how dreadful) castor oil to help the baby through the passage; she wanted to drink mint tea and wanted the after-birth planted under a tree here. She wanted folk things that I had never heard of. No caesarean section for her; she wanted to push out her baby herself and wanted it delivered by a local midwife. She, only having read about these things, was sure that a house-cleansing ceremony would clear away any bad spirits. When she actually got into the house, she declared that there were no bad spirits there. If they had been there before, they had vanished at her coming. It was then that I learnt that we in Jamaica were not the only people who had crazy ideas about the supernatural. Joy, for all her aristocratic look, had had a spiritual adviser right there in Washington, DC. He totally approved of her coming to me and she had been blessed with olive oil and even goat's blood and right there in the capital of the most significant country in Christendom's world.

I introduced her to the mat. In fact I told her it would be by her bedside. She sat on it, rolled on it and said, "This is what Vincent saw." This Vincent was her spiritual adviser, and she added, "The only thing I am to stay away from while I am here is the flesh of chickens." I thought I had told her about Nothing's revelation concerning my eating of the flesh of fowls but clearly I had not, so I told her and took the opportunity of introducing her to the people in the mat and their stories. My cousin was so taken with these stories that I was forced to remember that she was a writer and one with contacts who might publish our family story before I could get around to it. I got diplomatic and told her, "One day, after the baby and all that, we must get together on this project."

I don't walk barefooted. My aristocratic high-brown cousin did. You see, the earth has all sorts of beneficial properties; it is sacred – why else is it called Mother Earth. Pity and gratitude had sent me to visit Everard and I had found him in the same golden-age home in which he had put his father. At Easter, I would take Easter buns for him; at Christmas, chocolate tea and plait bread. With him I had walked out the "brother" part of the cemetery at the home. "Brother" is the euphemism for the part of the cemetery where those who really don't belong, whether by not being christened Anglican or by having been a charity case, are buried, and we did find Samuel's spot and the little marker that Everard had placed on it. So we were friends, but I hadn't managed to get him to come back to the house, which was now mine and which I supposed, from what he told me, held a lot of pain. It was on one of these days when this brown cousin of mine was walking with her planters and ten toes on the earth sucking up all the goodness from Mother Earth that Everard chose to visit. I saw the shock on his face and took him to my bench in the maze to regain his composure.

"It will be all right," he said. "It won't happen again."

And I knew what he was talking about. He had just seen his mother in her final days, brown like my cousin, in the flushed beauty of pregnancy, like my cousin, barefooted like my cousin and perhaps dressed like my cousin, for Joy did wear some long expensive-looking Indian-cotton outfits which looked just as out of step with my yard as those of Doris, daughter of Captain Smith, must have looked. I knew too that he would be praying to his Christian God for us and that all would be well. He asked questions: was she looking after herself? I knew what that meant and I could tell him that the seer never left us out and had even found a midwife for us. I didn't tell him, though, that I had gone further than that, for bush have ears and wall have eye. What I wasn't telling everyone was that I had found a gynecologist/obstetrician for my cousin. She was quite content with the midwife but I was not.

I am a Monday–Wednesday–Friday teacher and I took my cousin in with me on Fridays ostensibly to see her grandmother and to help with the groceries. The boy whose eyes used to follow me around was back and he was that gynecologist. I had to get Joy to believe that my taking her to Junior was a ploy for me to try my hand at getting him to notice me. He quite understood. Nevertheless things started to happen for us too, so that those Fridays on which he poked around in Joy's privates became days of peace, love and excitement for the three of us as lunch and laughter usually followed the gynecological examinations. Then another lovely thing materialized. His good friend, whom I knew only slightly, took to being part of our party. Junior felt that we shouldn't be driving so far out of town by ourselves on these Friday nights and his lawyer friend began accompanying him as he drove behind me to my house, twenty miles away from my college campus and our city. Sometimes we stopped on the road to eat; sometimes they ate at my house. Sometimes they even stayed over to enjoy the company of these weird cousins.

And the cousins got more weird. I have heard of men having a sympathetic reaction to the pregnancy of their wives. Never thought it would happen between friends and cousins and of the same sex. If you hadn't been told that my cousin was pregnant, and five months gone at that, you would not know, for the telltale sign of pregnancy, the big belly, was not a thing for Joy – though Everard, accustomed to seeing his mother pregnant, had guessed and correctly. All Joy had was a spread in her hips; but if like all of us you did not know how her hips were before, you couldn't even know that her hip-size had changed. We had to take her word for it that there was this new spread of the hip and that it was due to the making of her baby. I, on the other hand, was having difficulty getting my skirts to hook and my blouses were gaping at the front. It was Junior (stupid name for a big old doctor) who noticed the change in my body and laughingly said that I looked like I was in the early days of pregnancy. The weight wouldn't go off no matter how much walking I did, so it was I who looked pregnant. Looks were one thing.

I could manage that. What was a bother was the sleeping. Even in classes I was sleeping, so that my students were sorry for me and asking if the drive into school wasn't getting too much for me. They seemed to believe that I was indeed pregnant, certainly in some delicate physical condition.

Joy decided to help me. She was as qualified in teaching black history as I was and more popular than I, for several in Jamaica and among my students knew of her articles in *Ebony* and *Essence* and were very happy to have this personality in their programme. So here was the pregnant one full of energy and the non-pregnant one at home sleeping away, like the proverbial bear, hibernating. Junior said that every woman carried her pregnancy in her own way so it was not odd for Joy to be so active. The odd creature was me. I think I would have completely lost it if the nothing in my womb had taken to kicking me. This was the point at which we shifted, she finally showing the signs of pregnancy. And of course Joy was not quiet about it, motherhood being such a natural and happy community affair. Anybody's hand was invited to feel the kicking. Jeremiah was called in from his farming tasks to put his hand on Joy's belly and feel the kicking. And this child felt as if it were not just kicking but running down the football field and heading the ball. I was glad I was not asked to share this aspect of pregnancy. But I tell you, when the birthing time came around, it was I who was dilating. I shared this with Junior who took the opportunity of arriving at facts about my sex life which I didn't intend to reveal to him: what I was feeling was not dilating but a sexual craving, and he asked knowingly: "You mean you have never felt this before? My dear virgin, you are, as the man in the street would say, 'juicing'."

I made up my mind to say nothing more, but juicing or dilating, both he and the nana, Miss Cislyn, started asking about baby clothes and the arrangement of the room for the delivery. I was in the room for the birthing and I can tell you that I felt pain. I will not say that I felt as much as Joy, but I know I felt pain. Joy's daughter came out, was wrapped and, without being cleaned of all her blood, put on Joy's chest. All the pain left her face; I felt it continue in mine. Then the oddest thing happened. Have you ever peeled a tangerine and found at the top of the pegs a whole little set of tangerine pegs. This little set of pegs looks just like the normal set of pegs except for their size; they are about one hundredth the size of the real tangerine. It used to delight me to see this extra and little set. I used to call them the tangerine's baby. Joy's daughter was, they said, a normal eight-pounder. The after-birth would not come. As Miss Cislyn took the baby off Joy's body to clean it, she was shocked and disappointed to hear the good, mild and decent doctor blasphemously utter: "Backside. I cannot believe this," and order Joy to push again.

As if Joy were a pit, the two of them, Junior and Miss Cislyn, were peering into her now-distended privates and pressing the top of her stomach. Out came a little something no more than three pounds but crying as loudly when slapped as the eight-pounder had.

"I never expected this either," was of course Joy's comment, for she had noticed Junior's shock.

I was reminded of our grandmother's stories of her baking and how she would make miniatures of whatever orders she was filling, for her own children, John and Sally, who would put these on their own lata and she would stick this in the oven with her other things. Herbert had mentioned her doing this for him and Pauline, though Grandmother did not mention this to me. I suppose she wanted John's daughter, Joy, to feel special. Grandmother and her flirting again. And me and my jealousy again. Well, here was the miniature and I took Joy's comment in the same light: something specially arranged for the immature who can't do it all themselves.

"Princess, this is yours." She had taken to calling me Princess following Junior. Lucky she didn't know that sometimes under his breath it would be "Princess Virgin".

He joined in: "Princess. You have been carrying this pregnancy too. This is really yours."

Miss Cislyn said nothing. Looking after two babies was more rewarding financially than looking after one.

"But," I stumbled, "I am not prepared."

"Nonsense," said Junior. "I am here. Am I not to profit from this harvest? I have no children. This is the parson's cake." For Joy's sake, he explained.

"At every wedding, there is a special little cake sitting on top of the layers of cake. This one is for the officiating priest. He can take this and go away without the beauty of the real wedding cake being disturbed by cutting before time."

Joy breast-fed both babies for a time, then, true to Jamaican custom, the father, Junior, started arriving with store-bought food and of course clothes for our babies. He had suggested that I try breast-feeding but I refused to carry our weirdness this far, though my breasts did feel heavy and my blouses were again not able to be buttoned at the front. Junior was very often in the house. He had virtually moved in, for babies have to be walked about in the nights to stop them from crying and I was a working woman who had to be rested enough to drive twenty miles to work and back. Miss Cislyn was able to take Joy through all the folk things she wanted to experience, even asafoetida on the baby's hair. And of course she very early took the babies off store-bought food and they were drinking the juices of the fruits and vegetables coming from Jeremiah's efforts on my land. Our boy didn't go through all the folk things through which Joy ushered her daughter, but he still grew, and by leaps and bounds. By the time he was three months old, he was the same weight as his sister.

Three months! Joy had been with us for nine. It was about time for her to go back. This is where Bertie, Junior's friend, the lawyer, got his chance to become involved in the business of the weird cousins. It was no secret to him that the arrangement between Joy and me had been that I would register the baby, *one* as we had thought it would be, in my name and Joy would adopt it and take it home. That there were two didn't change anything. Bertie did the legal work and before long Joy had a birth certificate making Youlande hers by adoption. Neville and Pearl thought that we were mad, but as we pointed out to them, the whole family was mad. We were just carrying on the tradition. Pearl of course wanted to know something I had never thought of asking.

"Who is the real father of Youlande?"

I loved Joy's answer.

"God." To Grandmother's look of shock, she said: "Why can't my child be conceived by immaculate conception?"

I had put two and two together and was quite sure that Joy's lover was one of those extreme black professors who was locked away at the state's pleasure in some US jail. Poor Bertie could not compete, and though he was quite willing, nay eager, to join our crazy family as the husband of Joy and father of Youlande, Joy was giving him no encouragement at all.

12. the joyless village

We would miss Joy. She had been as good as her name. My place was no longer the haunted house with the strange woman living there; it now looked like the community centre, for there were children and a few adults all over the place every evening. Joy was, as they say in the country of her birth, "easy on the eyes", easier, I think, than I, but it was not just features. Joy was joy. She attracted all these people like ants to sugar. And she had this boundless energy. I would come home to find her playing hopscotch with the little girls or shooting marbles with the boys. Or a long line of adults and children, with Joy at the head, "stringing my needle". Singing, "*Thread, O, mi thread, O / Mi long long thread / Show me how you string your needle / Long, long thread.*" I was surprised that though she had spent her youth in the United States, she knew so many of the games that the children played here and that I and my age group had played. Then there was clapping: they taught each other nonsense words while they patted the body and did some intricate figures and patterns, looking like the square dancing I had learnt in high school. She would surely be missed.

It didn't totally end with her return to the States, but what was left was not real Joy. I am me and can't help thinking of getting the children ready for life, thus I was on to homework and my house was now a homework centre. Parents loved this, but not the children. "Love" is not the right word. "Approved" is better, for no one would be such a liar as to say that they didn't love the games session which Joy had led and were not sorry to see them go.

Our relationship – Joy's and mine – was not as nice as it was before she came to me. Our cooling off had something to do with Nothing's mat. Joy wanted me to send the mat to her so she could add our experiences to it. I couldn't let Nothing's mat out of my house. I thought that such a thing she shouldn't even have asked but I guess since I had left it in her room for all the time she was here, she probably did not know how much I cared about it. Same old story: stretch yourself for others and they think that you are a rubber band. I had not made her understand the sacrifice I was making in leaving the mat by her bed. In any case, as I tried to tell her, she could add nothing to the mat. The structures were there and all we would be doing through our lives was replicating them: the two women so close, you'd think they were sisters. She and I were just a repeat of Nothing and Pearl. And it was not just sisters. Look at John and Sally. They were so close that Sally's son John was John the second, not just the nephew but the namesake of John the first. John and Sally were as close as Polly and Herbert were. Then there were the childless ones – Nothing and Polly, and I suppose I.

Perhaps this is what hurt Joy. Hadn't she given me Modibe? Modibe, whom I feared, given our family's style of repeating lives, was destined to be John the second, and Evan, my own brother. My brother was languishing in prison in England for the same reasons that her John had been imprisoned in Virginia – for being black in a white country. That imprisonment had kept my parents in prison in England. They could not leave for any protracted time. Any day now, Evan would be released and they had to be home to welcome him; that was their eternal mantra. Not a peep of this to Neville and Pearl: they would die believing that Herbert did not care enough about them or me to really follow through on his promises and spend a long visit with us in Jamaica –something more than the little two weeks that he gave us. Could Modibe and I escape this, our black brothers' and sons' fate?

Joy was slow to respond. Her response came in a letter with a Georgia postmark rather than a Washington, DC, one. Joy had moved to a small college in Georgia. Now, for matters to bear such fruit so quickly, she had to have been planning that move from when she was with me in Jamaica. And not a word to me! I knew there was a maximum-security prison nearby and I could imagine that she would want to be close to her baby's father. But all of this was unaided invention on my part. It felt like lack of trust to me. I didn't say it but I felt it and was hurt. She complained that my letters were now dry facts. I didn't tell her that I would no longer be trusting my emotions to her. I didn't even tell her that Junior had convinced me that he could be a better father if he was husband of Modibe's mother. She would have loved the reasoning and laughed with all the joy inside of her.

"Princess Virgin," he said, "there are things you need to feel but at your age only a gynecologist can get you to feel them. Here I am. This is your last chance."

I took it. I knew it wouldn't change anything. Aunt Polly came out for my occasion. Junior sponsored her. It was Aunt Polly, he said, who had kept him in the family. When I was so busy with my iterations that I could not return his glances; it was Aunt Polly who would telephone him to find out how he was doing and to give him news of me. In a word, Aunt Polly did my courting for me.

Everard managed to make it to the event. I saw him looking at her and hoped that she would look back at him. Vain hope. I saw no such thing. My vulgar husband said that Everard would need a pick-axe to deal with her. I made it known to him that whatever happened, the house and land which came from Everard through Nothing to me, would be going to Aunt Polly. That was not a problem, for though he liked my house, he said, he would prefer to take us to his own and have me put my decorating skills on something which was his and which would come to me eventually. We got something in the Town near enough to Neville and Pearl, the burdens of whom he helped to share.

Joy wrote back. She apologized for being so insensitive. In the little university town in which she lives everybody does craft work in straw. It is quite a profession for some, and a hobby for others, people like her, I suppose, who have jobs. She was in the process of acquiring this skill, and remembering the mat at her bedside and its spiritual strength, she was carried away into thinking that she could add to the beauty and spirituality of the mat her American experiences. I was told that Victor thanked me and sent his love. Who was Victor? I assumed that that was the name of the father of my child. I wrote back to tell her of my wedding and to have her tell Victor that there was a place here for him to holiday whenever he felt like it and that I would be expecting Joy to come visit Modibe and Victor was welcome to come along with her.

Junior and I operated two homes. It was the Kingston home that got the centre table. I couldn't leave it alone. It was a highly polished mahogany one. This was where the pictures of Youlande, the world's most photographed baby, rested. I didn't need to post her picture in the country home in which she was born for there were several pictures of her all about the village. I wondered if there wasn't some chemical in cameras that would be bad for babies. I kept that thought to myself and made up my mind that Modibe would be photographed only every six months. I would have preferred if he wasn't photographed at all. There were healthier ways, I thought, of marking the development of a child for posterity. It wouldn't be a mat. I thought of a tree, then thought again that a tape measure and some words would be just as good. The photographing was so Joy could see what she had nurtured and given to me.

I sent a photograph of Modibe to Joy and her response threw me. She sent back to say that Modibe was the spitting image of his father. Again I was accusing Joy of insensitivity. Since Modibe was mine, I felt only I could talk about his father with the assurance I was hearing in Joy's words. It was my business whether Junior was Modibe's father, or her Victor's. What if Victor should come along and in one way or the other claim the boy? This thought frightened me and sent me again to Bertie, the lawyer, who assured me that in every legal way Modibe was mine and that with Junior officially adopting him, Modibe was safe in our arms. And the little boy was so "moreish".

I started sleeping again in class. My students teased me but I knew that the next thing on my woman's calendar was menopause and hot flashes. Along with the sleeping was a weight problem. You know the little black dress that goes everywhere and is so expensive? It refused to zip for the vice chancellor's annual dinner. My period had been playing hide and seek for some time now. "No trouble," the doctor, Junior's colleague whom he got to see me, had said. "This is normal. It only means that you are peri-menopausal." But he hadn't said that I was not to share my body with my duly anointed husband. I was frightened at the possibility that the dear doctor's mind had ruled out pregnancy. I had heard that old women produced albinos and children with like defects.

The child came – not like Joy's. It was taken. It was a girl. I vowed to give Clarise (the end sounding like "*ease* your body") the second a chance to live a normal and happy life this time.

13. victor

I might have been snubbing Joy, but she certainly was not snubbing me. She came for my birthing and brought her family with her. We had some honest talks. I was very glad for them. We were jealous of each other, we agreed. I was also, though I didn't tell her so, very pleased that Joy could be jealous of me. We kissed and made up and moved on to deciding what to tell our children about their origin. I suggested that we tell them the truth. In this day of test tube babies and surrogate mothers, their origins were fairly normal.

My problem, which I shared with Junior and of course not with Joy, was that I did not like my child's biological father. "Did not like"? I detested him and wished to see the back of him. Junior's suggestion was that we hold our noses and try to like him, for after all the guy wasn't staying forever: he'd soon be crawling back to whatever stone he has escaped from. The image was right. Joy's husband reminded you of a white cockroach stumbling to freedom after somebody's toe has accidentally upturned a stone. Prejudice aired, I had now to take thought and the thought that came was that Victor's colour was not odd to Joy, indeed must have been normal, because, as I had before concluded, for her to be so pale-skinned compared to me, Pearlie's first husband, her grandfather, must have been as near-white as this chap, and called and treated as black, or "silver" as it was in those days, only because he was American. I was forced too to see the union between Joy and Victor as the repeating pattern which was the story of our family and which would no doubt continue in our line given the speed with which barriers were now being broken.

Victor was in his mid-sixties to our mid-forties. He didn't know about cricket and they were here in the cricket season. Sabina Park was where the action was for Junior and his pals at this time of the year. Who wants to be explaining about "silly mid-on" and "gully" or why they play in white, when the last pair on your side, not known for their skill at batting, are in and there are twenty runs between a win and a loss? And he was very loud with his ignorant questions. Was this "gully" related to "Gully-Gaza disputes"? He had been following it and "Heh, heh, those boys were something else, weren't they?" Junior and his friends and those in their stand had zilch interest in Gully-Gaza issues, which Victor had clearly studied as a potential conversation piece and now felt that the time had come to show off.

And they said he was very slow on the draw. He just did not understand that where four men are drinking and three have already ordered and paid, you the fourth must now man up and order. Victor was attracted to patties. He could excuse himself and go off and eat a patty all by himself without asking anyone if he could get them one. It was different when Joy was around. But not all that less embarrassing.

We were taking them around the island. He couldn't help but see how much the gas bill was when we stopped to fill up. We later stopped to buy lunch by the wayside. No big cost. Three hundred dollars per plate. Joy asked us what we wanted, ordered and asked Victor to come help her take the plates to the car. We could hear his voice as he asked her, "Why buy four when there is just you and me. I can't eat two plates, nor can you."

I heard Joy say, "This is how it goes in this culture. If you are in a party, you share."

You have to say on his behalf that he took her point and shut up. But I didn't feel like eating their food. My fish and bammy, usually a delight, tasted like the ashes that the sinful ate in Milton's *Paradise Lost*. I hoped that Modibe would soon give up this quadroon look, would dark up fast, lose the big round face and stop looking like this man. Mulatto he would have to be, given his genes – but please, God, could You let him look, at most, sambo?

Behaviour is not genetically determined, for that I gave thanks knowing that I needn't fear that my child would be as strange as this man.

He loved his Joy, though. Joy had still not given me the slightest information on this cockroach, this unfortunate mixed-race lump of flesh that she had brought into my family. It was said oddity who enlightened me. I am grateful to him. Victor had not been in prison. He was no activist. He had merely been imprisoned in a marriage with a "white woman" who did not want to let him go. There was something unfortunate about this, I thought, since he wanted nothing but a straight-haired wig to pass as white. It was through Joy, whom he had met at a demonstration against the purge of some Howard faculty, that he had come to claim his blackness: "My mother was white, you know. My father, like so many black men, vanished leaving her to rear by herself a brown-skinned child. She did what she could. My paternal grandparents did not exist either so there was no one to teach me how to be black, until Joy came along."

Apparently he got his divorce and moved away from the marital home to this small college in Georgia while Joy was in Jamaica having his babies. He was ready for her with home, marriage officer and a job in the same college when she returned with Youlande in his "only child". I was so relieved to hear him talk about Youlande this way. Victor's occasional attempt at a joke was his apology for Modibe's colour. We laughed that off as often as we were required to, and I was satisfied that my child was that of Junior and me. Then I moved on to worrying about the difference in colour of my children and how I would explain this to them. The other three laughed so heartily at my fear that I was able to get over it and to simply watch my daughter as she developed into beautiful, intelligent and creative Clarise, pet-named Polly.

14. clarise the second

My husband thinks that I should be careful about favouritism. He thinks that I spend more time with Clarise than I should and less with Modibe than I should, but even he can see that in spite of this, the boy dotes on his little sister and helps me to pamper her. Junior finds it strange that Modibe, instead of being jealous, is supportive of my relationship with his sister: I of course do not. This closeness of siblings is a very pattern in my crazy family. I am no authority on children, not even having a niece or nephew, poor Evan's early child-bearing life being spent under the watchful eye of Her Majesty's guards, but I say with strong conviction that my daughter is an unusually blessed child. I early introduced her to Nothing's mat. She met all her relatives. By the time she was three she could recognize their places on the mat and took to talking with them. Perhaps they spoke to her or perhaps I just told her more than I can remember telling her. Whatever. She knew her people and I think was incorporating into herself the best of what there was in them. She, like Modibe, knew quite early about her relationship to fowls and we did keep fowls. They were her friends. She named them all. She could be heard apologizing to them as she collected their eggs.

Like every little middle-class girl in Jamaica, Clarise does dancing lessons. She is drawn towards perfection, and in dancing, as with all her endeavours, she practises hard. It was while she was practising her dancing that I was blown away. I had once been privileged to see Nothing in a pose which I felt was impossible, a skill that Nothing didn't want spoken about. I have never mentioned it to anyone, yet here was this child contorted like the bird into which I had seen Nothing turn herself, the bird into which Clarise's grandmother, the African, had perhaps turned herself to fly away home to wherever, and about which Clarise had told Nothing when she was just a baby. I asked her dancing teacher if she had taught her this move. She had not, but did think it remarkable. She had written a little ballet about the birth of Jesus in which there was a wide variety of non-human beings in the manger rejoicing at His birth. Five-year-old Clarise was the hen and choreographed her part, looking, her teacher said, for all the world like a real bird. What was this about? Clarise was also, somehow, Nothing. In her the circle was complete: the end was linked with the beginning and was even the beginning. With prayers she would be able to transcend whatever pains and hurts the earlier ones had faced.

With Clarise I have become one of the photograph-senders in the family. She joins her cousins on the centre table in the several houses in which our relatives lives, but it is only Joy to whom I sent the photograph of Clarise as a bird in that Christmas pantomime. She found it remarkable enough to share with Vincent. I had not forsaken my own seer, Robert. Both men found what they saw extraordinary and felt that I had produced an exceptional medium. They were both willing to take care of her.

Junior started to sound like my mother, cursing my family for its oddity, which we had inserted into his daughter. As he had to admit, nothing was happening that he didn't know about when he was gazing at me. Of course he has no fear that she will be protected from orthodox things: he is a doctor and has friends who are also physicians. There are among our very good friends many lawyers. There is help all around. We have nothing to fear from temporal powers. The spiritual is something else. What I have to do is pray that she will be able to manage the spiritual legacy that is hers.

My seer, whom she called and still calls Bobert, not having been able as a baby to say "Robert", visits often and talks with her. What Maud and in particular Clarise went through was no stroll in the park. I can see the pain in her when she touches their part of the mat. It can't be helped, Robert says, and talks her through the past experiences. Her father once listened in on their sessions. He had to admit that what he heard was no more or less than orthodox psychotherapy. Her brother, who knows the stories well, is intelligent enough to note bloodlines and feels sorry for his sister.

"Mom," he says, "some of these people aren't even our blood relations. How come Clarise has to feel their pain?" And he is right. I let him know that he is right, for Pearl, his great-grandmother, is only Nothing's cousin and that through her father. Their grandfather Herbert's line didn't pass through Maud and Clarise. They are not blood relations and his question I am eager to answer, for my children, given their circumstances, need to have this answers.

"Modibe, when our people came to this part of the world from Africa we didn't come as blood relations. We didn't come as brothers and sisters and mothers and father already knowing and loving each other. We came as individuals without family and without friends, strangers in a strange place, and like all human beings, needing to love and be loved. In the absence of family, we loved anyone we could find and were grateful for the love that anybody gave to us. So we have a history of loving and being loved not because we are blood relations but because God has put us in each other's way and we find something in each other to preserve, admire and to care for. Maud and Clarise and Nothing and all those people in the mat love us, care for us and want to be loved and cared for by us. They are our family, like you and Clarise are family."

Nothing is secret. When he knows the truth, he will need that explanation. *Selah.*

But more. The little boy, my good little boy, turned to me and said, "Then all I can do is to help her feel and bear the pain." There and then I understood something that had been eluding me: Why would Nothing be the one to be blessed or otherwise with being able to take the shape of the bird and not Grandma Pearl, who had the sympathetic relationship with hens and whose death they had even taken? Simple. Very simple. We feel for each other and carry each other's pain and blessing so much so that if the designated one cannot or will not perform, we take on the task. Just so must we have cried and screamed when one of us fell beneath the lash, too weak to cry out for herself.

15. remaking the mat

Some people have unhappiness written into their DNA, Junior says, the dot becoming a large circle and infinitely larger as they age. That is word thrown at me, for he says I have a mat, an extraordinary mat, but am I satisfied? No. I fear that the mat might self-destruct, and before I even see a break in it I am ready to go off in search of the material to make a new one.

Like all people of our status, we have two cars. The wife drives the station wagon and drops the children off to school, to after-school activities and to Saturday classes. Yes. I drive the station wagon and have the children most of the time. We do the usual travelling that all people of our status do, but ours is more, for we have two houses and are constantly moving between them. Where should the mat live? I settle this question by putting the mat where we most often are: that is, in the car. The trunk has become a kind of nursery for the children. Books, crayons, toys are in the trunk with them, even a potty, and the children sleep and play on the mat. Occasionally we roll them in the mat, as Cleopatra did to smuggle herself into Caesar's presence. We roll them in the mat to take their sleeping forms into one house or the other.

With all the lifting and playing, the mat is no longer stiff; it is now as pliable as cloth and some of the units are out of shape. I suspect that this is the beginning of unravelling. I have become accustomed to having the mat and the people it represented in my life. I do not want to have to be without them, which could happen if the mat did unravel and the units fell out. How would I manage? I think I could remake the mat and am thinking about where to find the triffid-like plant so that I can repeat the process. What's wrong with this thinking? I am only being proactive. Since Conut, I have never seen that plant. I suspect that with progress this plant had been cut down, perhaps to make space for apartment buildings and town houses.

When I talk about my projections for remaking the mat, Junior takes the mat and with his hands pulls in both directions to show how strong it is and to make his point that I am pursuing a non-issue. Which relative is he pulling? I wonder. My bright hopeful children who cringe with me when he pulls the mat say that the people in the mat will find the plant for me should anything happen to it, for they want to be with us as much as we want to be with them. I let this satisfy me. "For now," my husband says and kisses his children in gratitude. I think the debate is finished and my mind has gone into the bush looking for plants which are "natural", which follow the 1, 1, 2, 3, 5 recursion which Nothing attributed to the plant, the one which gave us the sisal for the mat. There must be another like it, I am thinking as I search the bush in my head, when I hear him.

"You know what you need?" and without waiting for my answer, his own comes: "Another child or two."

I have my response at the tip of my tongue that will end the talk and give me the conversational victory. "I am not Sarah and you are not God."

But there is more. "What about adoption. From what you have told me, that too is in your family. And though I am glad that no one thought us less than normal and thought to ask if my parents were my birth parents, I am like your mother. How come there is no mat about that and about her?" He is right, and I am silent. That is my mother's story, which has yet to be told. And am I so self-centred that I didn't inquire into Junior's past? Though I suppose that like my mother he has nobody to hand down his story. In any case, how would they fit into Nothing's mat? Would their story require a new mat? That is my children's story, I think. Still, it mightn't need another mat, for the children span the two sides. Where would this beginning be and where the end? I am thinking around this so I am very quiet. Junior does not trust my quietness.

"Couldn't I have shut my big mouth?" he asks himself. "Here we go. Another set of recursions and iterations."

This will be very difficult, I am thinking, for we know so little and I doubt that my mother or his parents want the little that they know aired. Still, the abandonment and adoption are part of the pattern, part of our truth and as such need to be known. The children will find a way of expressing this, I know, even if it means finding another heaven-blessed plant, making it into strings, shaping these strings into circles with their own recursions and iterations. The experience will certainly connect them to another set of kin and another set of happy energy. They won't know the nothingness that set me to completing Nothing's mat, because they understand more about ancestral spirits and energy than I knew at thirty. I do feel that I have accomplished something: I have set them off on the right path.

CPSIA information can be obtained
at www.ICGtesting.com
Printed in the USA
BVOW08s0710090417
480735BV00001B/78/P